# AUNT JANE'S NIECES

### By
### L. FRANK BAUM
### Writing As
### EDITH VAN DYNE

ANTIOCII, CALIFORNIA
## THE INTERNATIONAL
## WIZARD OF OZ CLUB
PUBLISHERS

Printed in the United States of America by
INTERNATIONAL WIZARD OF OZ CLUB, INC.
1407 A Street, Suite D, Antioch, CA 94509

ISBN 1-930764-09-X

For more information about our publications
please visit **www.ozclub.org**

Layout and Design by Marcus Mebes 2003

# AUNT JANE'S NIECES
## An Introduction

When I was asked to write an introduction for *Aunt Jane's Nieces*, I was at once reminded of a family story about the author, Edith Van Dyne. It took place several years after the first volume in the Aunt Jane's Nieces series came out in 1906. Mrs. Van Dyne's series had become quite popular with teenage girls. An eastern publisher, wishing to capitalize on this popularity, wrote to Mrs. Van Dyne, in care of her publisher, Reilly and Britton, to ask if he might be allowed to send a representative to meet with Mrs. Van Dyne. He was in hopes that Mrs. Van Dyne would write for his publication.

Reilly and Britton in no way wanted to inform the publisher that Edith Van Dyne was, in reality, L. Frank Baum, famous for his Oz books. They also did not want to give any hints that Edith Van Dyne did not exist, so they suggested that the representative from the eastern publisher meet with Mrs. Van Dyne for tea at a hotel in Syracuse, New York, Mrs. Van Dyne's "home town."

A staff author for Reilly and Britton was given the job of representing herself as "Mrs. Van Dyne" for the interview. She was carefully coached after reading all of the Aunt Jane's Nieces books which had been published to date. It just so happened that at the same time the eastern publisher representative was supposed to meet with Mrs. Van Dyne, the Baums were visiting

ii AUNT JANE'S NIECES

relatives in the Syracuse area, and so they joined Mrs. Van Dyne at the tea. To complete the scene, the staff author was introduced to the representative as Mrs. Van Dyne and the Baums were introduced under assumed names. When the tea ended, the representative from the eastern publisher had been thoroughly charmed and duped. Needless to say, Mrs. Van Dyne turned down the opportunity to write for the eastern publisher and he was therefore unable to secure her services.

One can only imagine what must have gone on at the tea or perhaps what hints or comments L. Frank might have said that could have "tipped" the representative off as to the true identity of Mrs. Van Dyne. I sincerely doubt that L. Frank could have passed up an opportunity to question the author posing as Mrs. Van Dyne. Maud, L. Frank's wife, must have had a good laugh at the whole thing too. Another family version of that same incident has Maud being coached by L. Frank to play the part of Mrs. Van Dyne at the interview. Regardless, I suppose you could say that "Frank had his cake and was 'Edith' too!"

Edith Van Dyne and her series were born on October 6, 1905 in a contract between L. Frank Baum and Reilly and Britton The fourth stipulation of that contract states:

*Fourth: Baum shall deliver to The Reilly and Britton Co. on or before March 1, 1906 the manuscript of a book for young girls on the*

# INTRODUCTION    iii

*style of the Louisa M. Alcott stories, but not
so good, the authorship to be ascribed to "Ida
May McFarland," or to "Ethel Lynne" or
some other mythological female.*

It appears that L. Frank had a hand in the writing
of this contract and most likely came up with the pseud-
onym, Edith Van Dyne, himself. Perhaps the name
came from his imagination or some person or persons
he knew. No one in the family has any information
that would shed light on the origin of the name.

Perhaps even more intriguing than Edith Van
Dyne's beginning or the family story, is the fact that
Edith Van Dyne's true identity, L. Frank Baum, was
not known until sometime after Baum's death.

Reilly and Britton certainly kept up the illusion of
Mrs. Van Dyne with their publicity. In an early ad for
the first book, *Aunt Jane's Nieces*, the story is billed as
"A Fascinating Story for Girls." The ad further stated
the book was:

*A story of three girls who were invited by a
hitherto neglectful, but wealthy maiden aunt
to visit her home. The objective was no
secret—the aunt desired to choose one of her
nieces' to succeed to her large estate. The appearance of Uncle John, first thought to be
poor and afterwards found to be tremendously
rich, the finding of a will which defeated the
bequests of Aunt Jane, and the final rescue of*

*the nieces by Uncle John, makes fine reading
and points a moral without moralizing. The
author has an extraordinary chance in her
more than clever story to portray characters
and does it ingeniously.*

Another newspaper ad for *Aunt Jane's Nieces*,
which I found in Maud's scrapbook, appeared in a col-
umn marked "For Book Lovers." Unfortunately, it had
no date or newspaper name. It read:

*AUNT JANE'S NIECES*
*Which one of the three girls invited by their
maiden aunt to visit her at Elmhurst will inherit her wealth, is the theme of Edith Van
Dyne's book. Most readers who are told the
reason she invited them will discover the gold
under the surface of one of these three characters and will make a pretty close guess as to
the legatee. But it won't do for us to say what
we guessed, for that would spoil the reading
for girls of one of the choice books for them of
the season. The very excellent thing about this
book is that the girls in its pages are just the
average girls. None of the sprout angel wings
and they are made to do what real, bona fide
girls in real life would do in like conditions.
We do not like teetotal goodness anymore than
we like teetotal badness. We all like a fair average. And in this book "Elizabeth," "Louise"*

*and "Patsy" are representative of that aver-
age. The introduction of "Uncle John," "Aunt
Jane's" brother and uncle to these girls, is a
clever bit of the scheme and plays an important role in the final settlement of the affair—
particularly as it relates to the boy "Kenneth."
If he didn't marry "Patsy" we shall never forgive him nor will any of the girl readers of
this clean, wholesome, natural character
study. A book of real worth. The Reilly and
Britton Co., Chicago.*

Like Dorothy in *The Wizard of Oz*, Van Dyne's
girls display independent thinking and unwillingness
to meekly stand by and let things happen to them. They
are a take-charge "modern woman" of Baum's—or
should I say Edith Van Dyne's—design. Perhaps this
new idea of what a woman should be is why the Aunt
Jane's Nieces series was very popular and outsold
Baum's books for boys.

By 1911 with six books in the series, L. Frank
Baum continued to write under the name of Edith Van
Dyne and started another series called *The Flying Girl*.
Van Dyne's portrayal of Orissa Kane, the heroine of
the Flying Girl stories, met with sharp resistance from
Reilly and Britton in the second of the series, *The Flying Girl and Her Chum*. Reilly and Britton felt that
there were a few things about Orissa Kane that made
her too exciting and sensational for women of that time.

In a reply to Reilly and Britton's letter on May 15, 1912, L. Frank writes:

*I am in receipt of your letter and wish to say that I consider the criticism of your reader in regards to "The Flying Girl and Her Chum," to be just and proper. I find I have a tendency to be ultra-sensational in these girls' books, and it is a fault I must earnestly try to correct. I suppose I have acquired that habit through writing fairy tales, where exaggeration is a virtue; so that when I get into this other class of stories, I am unconsciously tempted to create a plot too weird for the purposes I wish to accomplish. I will bear this in mind and try to tone down the excitement in future stories.*

Even though this letter was written years after he started the Aunt Jane's Nieces series, I feel it gives some insight into my great grandfather's thinking about the qualities he wanted his female characters to portray.

Throughout his career, my great grandfather derived many of his characters and situations from his own life and experiences. The Baum family has always looked on the Aunt Jane's Nieces series as somewhat autobiographical of L. Frank's life. In this case, you could say he was truly following the old adage of "write about what you know."

A number of these similarities are not hard to see in *Aunt Jane's Nieces*. The great estate of Elmhurst

and Jane's holdings in the area are a return to his childhood home, Rose Lawn and his father's land and oil
business in and around the Syracuse area. Baum's attention to the gardens and paths comes from these early
experiences as does Jane's love of fresh cut flowers in
the manor. His garden at "Ozcot" in Hollywood was
most likely modeled after these childhood memories
as well.

The character of Kenneth Forbes, from *Aunt Jane's
Nieces*, combines both L. Frank's feelings about his
early childhood and what he thought people around
him were most likely saying about him. Kenneth's lack
of a formal education mirrors Baum's. Silas Watson's
comment to Kenneth, "Money is very necessary to one
who is incompetent to earn his salt" is a lesson and a
moral to be learned by many. I am sure that this senti-
ment comes directly from L. Frank questioning his own
abilities after several failed endeavors caused him to
wonder whether he'd be able to "earn his salt."

I have been a teacher for thirty-three years (sorry,
L. Frank!) and I can fully understand my great
grandfather's disdain for teachers and institutions of
higher learning. Some tend to destroy childhood imagination and replace it with an abundance of useless information and elitism. My great grandfather somewhat
tempered his views on education. When Louise answers
Beth's question of "Have you graduated?" she says,
"No, it wasn't worth while... I'm sure I know as much

as most girls do, and there are more useful lessons to be learned from real life than from books." I feel that L. Frank had come to believe this last statement early on in his life.

In my personal collection, I have a set of Aunt Jane's Nieces books that L. Frank gave to his second son, Robert S. Baum, my grandfather, in 1916. Only a few of them are first editions but what makes them so interesting is what L. Frank wrote in them. In the first book he wrote, "When I wrote this I had no idea of making a series from it, but it 'caught on' and resulted in ten volumes." It is signed "Edith Van Dyne" with "L. Frank Baum" in parentheses under it. Each of the other volumes has some note indicating what part of his life he was writing about. My grandfather always felt that his father liked the series and enjoyed writing them.

The Aunt Jane's Nieces series turned out to be a financial success for L. Frank. He even referred to it as "his bread and butter series." Reilly and Britton Co. felt the same way and put a great deal of thought into the marketing of the series. They stressed to L. Frank the importance of having each new book ready for the spring promotional push. By the ninth book, the publishers were claiming that the series was one of the three best selling girls series in the world. Whether this was true or not, the series sold well and was available from the publisher as late as 1926.

In the June 24, 1911 issue of *The Publishers' Weekly*, a Baum/Edith Van Dyne connection did occur. The connection came in the form of a full-page ad for The Flying Girl. At the top of the page was a picture taken by L. Frank Baum of his garden at "Ozcot." Under the picture appears the following caption:

*Above is a picture of L. Frank Baum's home and gardens at Hollywood, California. In the center of the pergola is the little sheltered garden house where EDITH VAN DYNE, a guest of Mrs. Baum, wrote THE FLYING GIRL. A book for young folks, 12 to 18 years. This is a most exciting story, and probably the best she ever wrote— which is saying much when we take into consideration that Mrs. Van Dyne is the author of "Aunt Jane's Nieces" and five other titles comprising that "Aunt Jane" Series. She has a way in all of her stories of setting forth the REAL doings of REAL girls and boys.*

*THE FLYING GIRL is published in most attractive 12mo form at $1.00 net. It is an up-to-the-minute story for girls particularly, but boys will also find it capital reading. While full of thrills and adventures, the book is clean and wholesome and can be recommended by dealers.*

I am positive that L. Frank was, once again, playing with his readers and publisher. I bet he had a big grin on his face as he sent this ad off to be printed. I also wish we could buy the book for the dollar as advertised!

I hope I have shed some light on the elusive Mrs. Edith Van Dyne and her renowned books, so full of REAL doings for REAL girls. I also hope you get as much enjoyment out of reading the series as I think my great grandfather had in writing them.

Ozily yours,

Robert A. Baum

# A LIST OF CHAPTERS

# CHAPTER I.

Professor De Graf was sorting the mail at the breakfast table.

"Here's a letter for you, Beth," said he, and tossed it across the cloth to where his daughter sat.

The girl raised her eyebrows, expressing surprise. It was something unusual for her to receive a letter. She picked up the square envelope between a finger and thumb and carefully read the inscription, "Miss Elizabeth De Graf, Cloverton, Ohio." Turning the envelope she found on the reverse flap a curious armorial emblem, with the word "Elmhurst."

Then she glanced at her father, her eyes big and somewhat startled in expression. The Professor was deeply engrossed in a letter from Ben-

9

jamin Lowenstein which declared that a certain note must be paid at maturity. His weak, watery blue eyes stared rather blankly from behind the gold-rimmed spectacles. His flat nostrils extended and compressed like those of a frightened horse; and the indecisive mouth was tremulous. At the best the Professor was not an imposing personage. He wore a dressing-gown of soiled quilted silk and linen not too immaculate; but his little sandy moustache and the goatee that decorated his receding chin were both carefully waxed into sharp points—an indication that he possessed at least one vanity. Three days in the week he taught vocal and instrumental music to the ambitious young ladies of Cloverton. The other three days he rode to Pelham's Grove, ten miles away, and taught music to all who wished to acquire that desirable accomplishment. But the towns were small and the fees not large, so that Professor De Graf had much difficulty in securing an income sufficient for the needs of his family.

The stout, sour-visaged lady who was half-hidden by her newspaper at the other end of the table was also a bread-winner, for she taught embroidery to the women of her acquaintance and made various articles of fancy-work that were sold at Biggar's Emporium, the largest store in Cloverton. So, between them, the Professor and Mrs. De Graf managed to defray ordinary expenses and keep Elizabeth at school; but there were one or two dreadful "notes" that were constantly hanging over their heads like the sword of Damocles, threatening to ruin them at any moment their creditors proved obdurate.

Finding her father and mother both occupied, the girl ventured to open her letter. It was written in a sharp, angular, feminine hand and read as follows:

"My Dear Niece: It will please me to have you spend the months of July and August as my guest at Elmhurst. I am in miserable health, and wish to become better acquainted with you before I die. A check for necessary expenses is enclosed and I shall expect you to arrive promptly on the first of July.

Your Aunt,

JANE MERRICK."

A low exclamation from Elizabeth caused her father to look in her direction. He saw the bank check lying beside her plate and the sight lent an eager thrill to his voice.

"What is it, Beth?"

"A letter from Aunt Jane."

Mrs. De Graf gave a jump and crushed the newspaper into her lap.

"What!" she screamed.

"Aunt Jane has invited me to spend two months at Elmhurst," said Elizabeth, and passed the letter to her mother, who grabbed it excitedly.

"How big is the check, Beth?" enquired the Professor, in a low tone.

"A hundred dollars. She says it's for my expenses.

"Huh! Of course you won't go near that dreadful old cat, so we can use the money to better advantage."

"Adolph!"

The harsh, cutting voice was that of his wife, and the Professor shrank back in his chair.

"Your sister Jane is a mean, selfish, despicable

old female," he muttered. "You've said so a thousand times yourself, Julia."

"My sister Jane is a very wealthy woman, and she's a Merrick," returned the lady, severely. "How dare you—a common De Graf—asperse her character?"

"The De Grafs are a very good family," he retorted.

"Show me one who is wealthy! Show me one who is famous!"

"I can't," said the Professor. "But they're decent, and they're generous, which is more than can be said for your tribe."

"Elizabeth must go to Elmhurst," said Mrs. De Graf. ignoring her husband's taunt.

"She shan't. Your sister refused to loan me fifty dollars last year, when I was in great trouble. She hasn't given you a single cent since I married you. No daughter of mine shall go to Elmhurst to be bullied and insulted by Jane Merrick."

"Adolph, try to conceal the fact that you're a fool," said his wife. "Jane is in a desperate state of health, and can't live very long at the best. I

13

believe she's decided to leave her money to Elizabeth, or she never would have invited the child to visit her. Do you want to fly in the face of Providence, you doddering old imbecile?"

"No," said the Professor, accepting the doubtful appellation without a blush. "How much do you suppose Jane is worth?"

"A half million, at the very least. When she was a girl she inherited from Thomas Bradley, the man she was engaged to marry, and who was suddenly killed in a railway accident, more than a quarter of a million dollars, besides that beautiful estate of Elmhurst. I don't believe Jane has even spent a quarter of her income, and the fortune must have increased enormously. Elizabeth will be one of the wealthiest heiresses in the country!"

"If she gets the money, which I doubt," returned the Professor, gloomily.

"Why should you doubt it, after this letter?"

"You had another sister and a brother, and they both had children," said he.

"They each left a girl, I admit. But Jane has never favored them any more than she has me.

14

And this invitation, coming when Jane is practically on her death bed, is a warrant that Beth will get the money."

"I hope she will," sighed the music teacher. "We all need it bad enough, I'm sure."

During this conversation Elizabeth, who might be supposed the one most interested in her Aunt's invitation, sat silently at her place, eating her breakfast with her accustomed calmness of demeanor and scarcely glancing at her parents.

She had pleasant and quite regular features, for a girl of fifteen, with dark hair and eyes—the "Merrick eyes," her mother proudly declared—and a complexion denoting perfect health and colored with the rosy tints of youth. Her figure was a bit slim and unformed, and her shoulders stooped a little more than was desirable; but in Cloverton Elizabeth had the reputation of being "a pretty girl," and a sullen and unresponsive one as well.

Presently she rose from her seat, glanced at the clock, and then went into the hall to get her hat and school-books. The prospect of being an heiress some day had no present bearing on the fact that it was time to start for school.

Her father came to the door with the check in his hand.

"Just sign your name on the back of this, Beth," said he, "and I'll get it cashed for you."

The girl shook her head.

"No, father," she answered. "If I decide to go to Aunt Jane's I must buy some clothes; and if you get the money I'll never see a cent of it."

"When will you decide?" he asked.

"There's no hurry. I'll take time to think it over," she replied. "I hate Aunt Jane, of course; so if I go to her I must be a hypocrite, and pretend to like her, or she never will leave me her property.

"Well, Beth?"

"Perhaps it will be worth while; but if I go into that woman's house I'll be acting a living lie."

"But think of the money!" said her mother.

"I do think of it. That's why I didn't tell you at once to send the check back to Aunt Jane. I'm going to think of everything before I decide. But if I go—if I allow this money to make me a hypocrite—I won't stop at trifles, I assure you. It's in my nature to be dreadfully wicked and cruel and selfish, and perhaps the money isn't worth the risk I run of becoming depraved."

"Elizabeth!"

"Good-bye; I'm late now," she continued, in the same quiet tone, and walked slowly down the walk.

The Professor twisted his moustache and looked into his wife's eyes with a half frightened glance.

"Beth's a mighty queer girl," he muttered.

"She's very like her Aunt Jane," returned Mrs. De Graf, thoughtfully gazing after her daughter. "But she's defiant and wilful enough for all the Merricks put together. I do hope she'll decide to go to Elmhurst."

# CHAPTER II.

In the cosy chamber of an apartment located in a fashionable quarter of New York Louise Merrick reclined upon a couch, dressed in a dainty morning gown and propped and supported by a dozen embroidered cushions.

Upon a taboret beside her stood a box of bonbons, the contents of which she occasionally nibbled as she turned the pages of her novel.

The girl had a pleasant and attractive face, although its listless expression was singular in one so young. It led you to suspect that the short seventeen years of her life had robbed her of all the anticipation and eagerness that is accustomed to pulse in strong young blood, and filled her with experiences that compelled her to accept ex-

18

istence in a half bored and wholly matter-of-fact way.

The room was tastefully though somewhat elaborately furnished; yet everything in it seemed as fresh and new as if it had just come from the shop—which was not far from the truth. The apartment itself was new, with highly polished floors and woodwork, and decorations undimmed by time. Even the girl's robe, which she wore so gracefully, was new, and the books upon the center-table were of the latest editions.

The portiere was thrust aside and an elderly lady entered the room, seating herself quietly at the window, and, after a single glance at the form upon the couch, beginning to embroider patiently upon some work she took from a silken bag. She moved so noiselessly that the girl did not hear her and for several minutes absolute silence pervaded the room.

Then, however, Louise in turning a leaf glanced up and saw the head bent over the embroidery. She laid down her book and drew an open letter from between the cushions beside her, which she languidly tossed into the other's lap.

"Who is this woman, mamma?" she asked.

Mrs. Merrick glanced at the letter and then read it carefully through, before replying.

"Jane Merrick is your father's sister," she said, at last, as she thoughtfully folded the letter and placed it upon the table.

"Why have I never heard of her before?" enquired the girl, with a slight accession of interest in her tones.

"That I cannot well explain. I had supposed you knew of your poor father's sister Jane, although you were so young when he died that it is possible he never mentioned her name in your presence."

"They were not on friendly terms, you know. Jane was rich, having inherited a fortune and a handsome country place from a young man whom she was engaged to marry, but who died on the eve of his wedding day."

"How romantic!" exclaimed Louise.

"It does seem romantic, related in this way," replied her mother. "But with the inheritance all romance disappeared from your aunt's life. She became a crabbed, disagreeable woman, old before her time and friendless because she suspected everyone of trying to rob her of her money. Your poor father applied to her in vain for assistance, and I believe her refusal positively shortened his life. When he died, after struggling bravely to succeed in his business, he left nothing but his life-insurance."

"Thank heaven he left that!" sighed Louise.

"Yes; we would have been beggared, indeed, without it," agreed Mrs. Merrick. "Yet I often wonder, Louise, how we managed to live upon the interest of that money for so many years."

"We didn't live—we existed," corrected the girl, yawning. "We scrimped and pinched, and denied ourselves everything but bare necessities. And had it not been for your brilliant idea, mater dear, we would still be struggling in the depths of poverty."

Mrs. Merrick frowned, and leaned back in her chair.

"I sometimes doubt if the idea was so brilliant, after all," she returned, with a certain grimness of expression. "We're plunging, Louise; and it may be into a bottomless pit."

# AUNT JANE'S NIECES.

"Don't worry, dear," said the girl, biting into a bonbon. "We are only on the verge of our great adventure, and there's no reason to be discouraged yet, I assure you. Brilliant! Of course the idea was brilliant, mamma. The income of that insurance money was insignificant, but the capital is a very respectable sum. I am just seventeen years of age—although I feel that I ought to be thirty, at the least—and in three years I shall be twenty, and a married woman. You decided to divide our capital into three equal parts, and spend a third of it each year, this plan enabling us to live in good style and to acquire a certain social standing that will allow me to select a wealthy husband. It's a very brilliant idea, my dear! Three years is a long time. I'll find my Croesus long before that, never fear."

"You ought to," returned the mother, thoughtfully. "But if you fail, we shall be entirely ruined."

"A strong incentive to succeed." said Louise, smiling. "An ordinary girl might not win out; but I've had my taste of poverty, and I don't like it. No one will suspect us of being adventurers, for as long as we live in this luxurious fashion we shall pay our bills promptly and be proper and respectable in every way. The only chance we run lies in the danger that eligible young men may prove shy, and refuse to take our bait; but are we not diplomats, mother dear? We won't despise a millionaire, but will be content with a man who can support us in good style, or even in comfort, and in return for his money I'll be a very good wife to him. That seems sensible and wise, I'm sure, and not at all difficult of accomplishment."

Mrs. Merrick stared silently out of the window, and for a few moments seemed lost in thought.

"I think, Louise," she said at last, "you will do well to cultivate your rich aunt, and so have two strings to your bow."

"You mean that I should accept her queer invitation to visit her?"

"Yes."

"She has sent me a check for a hundred dollars. Isn't it funny?"

"Jane was always a whimsical woman. Per-

23

haps she thinks we are quite destitute, and fears you would not be able to present a respectable appearance at Elmhurst without this assistance. But it is an evidence of her good intentions. Finding death near at hand she is obliged to select an heir, and so invites you to visit her that she may study your character and determine whether you are worthy to inherit her fortune."

The girl laughed, lightly.

"It will be easy to cajole the old lady," she said. "In two days I can so win her heart that she will regret she has neglected me so long."

"Exactly."

"If I get her money we will change our plans, and abandon the adventure we were forced to undertake. But if, for any reason, that plan goes awry, we can fall back upon this prettily conceived scheme which we have undertaken. As you say, it is well to have two strings to one's bow; and during July and August everyone will be out of town, and so we shall lose no valuable time."

Mrs. Merrick did not reply. She stitched away in a methodical manner, as if abstracted, and Louise crossed her delicate hands behind her head and gazed at her mother reflectively. Presently she said:

"Tell me more of my father's family. Is this rich aunt of mine the only relative he had?"

"No, indeed. There were two other sisters and a brother—a very uninteresting lot, with the exception of your poor father. The eldest was John Merrick, a common tinsmith, if I remember rightly, who went into the far west many years ago and probably died there, for he was never heard from. Then came Jane, who in her young days had some slight claim to beauty. Anyway, she won the heart of Thomas Bradley, the wealthy young man I referred to, and she must have been clever to have induced him to leave her his money. Your father was a year or so younger than Jane, and after him came Julia, a coarse and disagreeable creature who married a music-teacher and settled in some out-of-the-way country town. Once, while your father was alive, she visited us for a few days, with her baby daughter, and nearly drove us all crazy. Perhaps she did not find us very hospitable, for we were too poor to

25

entertain lavishly. Anyway, she went away suddenly after you had a fight with her child and nearly pulled its hair out by the roots, and I have never heard of her since."

"A daughter, eh," said Louise, musingly. "Then this rich Aunt Jane has another niece besides myself."

"Perhaps two," returned Mrs. Merrick; "for her youngest sister, who was named Violet, married a vagabond Irishman and had a daughter about a year younger than you. The mother died, but whether the child survived her or not I have never learned."

"What was her name?" asked Louise.

"I cannot remember. But it is unimportant. You are the only Merrick of them all, and that is doubtless the reason Jane has sent for you."

The girl shook her blonde head.

"I don't like it," she observed.

"Don't like what?"

"All this string of relations. It complicates matters."

Mrs. Merrick seemed annoyed.

"If you fear your own persuasive powers,"

she said, with almost a sneer in her tones, "you'd better not go to Elmhurst. One or the other of your country cousins might supplant you in your dear aunt's affections."

The girl yawned and took up her neglected novel.

"Neverthereless, mater dear," she said briefly, "I shall go."

# CHAPTER III.

"Now, Major, stand up straight and behave yourself! How do you expect me to sponge your vest when you're wriggling around in that way?"

"Patsy, dear, you're so sweet this avening, I just had to kiss your lips."

"Don't do it again, sir," replied Patricia, severely, as she scrubbed the big man's waistcoat with a damp cloth. "And tell me, Major, how you ever happened to get into such a disgraceful condition."

"The soup just shpilled," said the Major, meekly.

Patricia laughed merrily. She was a tiny thing, appearing to be no more than twelve years old, although in reality she was sixteen. Her hair was a decided red—not a beautiful "auburn," but really red—and her round face was badly freckled. Her nose was too small and her mouth too wide to be beautiful, but the girl's wonderful blue eyes fully redeemed these faults and led the observer to forget all else but their fascinations. They could really dance, these eyes, and send out magnetic, scintillating sparks of joy and laughter that were potent to draw a smile from the sourest visage they smiled upon. Patricia was a favorite with all who knew her, but the big, white-moustached Major Doyle, her father, positively worshipped her, and let the girl rule him as her fancy dictated.

"Now, sir, you're fairly decent again," she said, after a few vigorous scrubs. "So put on your hat and we'll go out to dinner."

They occupied two small rooms at the top of a respectable but middle-class tenement building, and had to descend innumerable flights of bare wooden stairs before they emerged upon a narrow street thronged with people of all sorts and descriptions except those who were too far removed from the atmosphere of Duggan street to know that it existed.

The big major walked stiffly and pompously along, swinging his silver-trimmed cane in one hand while Patricia clung to his other arm. The child wore a plain grey cloak, for the evening was chill. She had a knack of making her own clothes, all of simple material and fashion, but fitting neatly and giving her an air of quiet refinement that made more than one passer-by turn to look back at her curiously.

After threading their way for several blocks they turned in at the open door of an unobtrusive restaurant where many of the round white tables were occupied by busy and silent patrons.

The proprietor nodded to the major and gave Patricia a smile. There was no need to seat them, for they found the little table in the corner where they were accustomed to eat, and sat down.

"Did you get paid tonight?" asked the girl.

"To be sure, my Patsy."

"Then hand over the coin," she commanded.

The major obeyed. She counted it carefully and placed it in her pocketbook, afterwards passing a half-dollar back to her father.

"Remember, Major, no riotous living! Make

AUNT JANE'S NIECES.

that go as far as you can, and take care not to
invite anyone to drink with you."

"Yes, Patsy."

"And now I'll order the dinner."

The waiter was bowing and smiling beside
her. Everyone smiled at Patsy, it seemed.

They gave the usual order, and then, after a
moment's hesitation, she added:

"And a bottle of claret for the Major."

Her father fairly gasped with amazement.

"Patsy!"

People at the near-by tables looked up as her
gay laugh rang out, and beamed upon her in
sympathy.

"I'm not crazy a bit, Major," said she, patting the hand he had stretched toward her, partly in delight and partly in protest. "I've just
had a raise, that's all, and we'll celebrate the occasion."

Her father tucked the napkin under his chin
then looked at her questioningly.

"Tell me, Patsy."

"Madam Borne sent me to a swell house on
Madison Avenue this morning, because all her

31

women were engaged. I dressed the lady's hair in my best style, Major, and she said it was much more becoming than Juliette ever made it. Indeed, she wrote a note to Madam, asking her to send me, hereafter, instead of Juliette, and Madam patted my head and said I would be a credit to her, and my wages would be ten dollars a week, from now on. Ten dollars, Major! As much as you earn yourself at that miserable bookkeeping!"

"Sufferin' Moses!" ejaculated the astonished major, staring back into her twinkling eyes. "If this kapes on, we'll be millionaires, Patsy."

"We're millionaires, now," responded Patsy, promptly, "because we've health, and love, and contentment—and enough money to keep us from worrying. Do you know what I've decided, Major, dear? You shall go to make that visit to your colonel that you've so long wanted to have. The vacation will do you good, and you can get away all during July, because you haven't rested for five years. I went to see Mr. Conover this noon, and he said he'd give you the month willingly, and keep the position for you when you returned."

"What! You spoke to old Conover about me?"

"This noon. It's all arranged, daddy, and you'll just have a glorious time with the old colonel. Bless his dear heart, he'll be overjoyed to have you with him, at last."

The major pulled out his handkerchief, blew his nose vigorously, and then surreptitiously wiped his eyes.

"Ah, Patsy, Patsy; it's an angel you are, and nothing less at all, at all."

"Rubbish, Major. Try your claret, and see if it's right. And eat your fish before it gets cold. I'll not treat you again, sir, unless you try to look happy. Why, you seem as glum as old Conover himself!"

The major was positively beaming.

"Would it look bad for me to kiss you, Patsy?"

"Now?"

"Now and right here in this very room!"

"Of course it would. Try and behave, like

the gentleman you are, and pay attention to your dinner!"

It was a glorious meal. The cost was twenty-five cents a plate, but the gods never feasted more grandly in Olympus than these two simple, loving souls in that grimy Duggan street restaurant.

Over his coffee the major gave a sudden start and looked guiltily into Patricia's eyes.

"Now, then," she said, quickly catching the expression, "out with it."

"It's a letter," said the major. "It came yesterday, or mayhap the day before. I don't just remember."

"A letter! And who from?" she cried, surprised.

"An ould vixen."

"And who may that be?"

"Your mother's sister Jane. I can tell by the emblem on the flap of the envelope," said he, drawing a crumpled paper from his breast pocket.

"Oh, *that* person," said Patsy, with scorn. "Whatever induced her to write to *me?*"

"You might read it and find out," suggested the major.

Patricia tore open the envelope and scanned the letter. Her eyes blazed.

"What is it, Mavoureen?"

"An insult!" she answered, crushing the paper in her hand and then stuffing it into the pocket of her dress. "Light your pipe, daddy, dear. Here—I'll strike the match."

# CHAPTER IV.

"How did you enjoy the reception, Louise?"

"Very well, mamma. But I made the discovery that my escort, Harry Wyndham, is only a poor cousin of the rich Wyndham family, and will never have a penny he doesn't earn himself."

"I knew that," said Mrs. Merrick. "But Harry has the entree into some very exclusive social circles. I hope you treated him nicely, Louise. He can be of use to us."

"Oh, yes, I think I interested him; but he's a very stupid boy. By the way, mamma, I had an adventure last evening, which I have had no time to tell you of before."

"Yes?"

"It has given me quite a shock. You no-

36

ticed the maid you ordered to come from Madam
Borne to dress my hair for the reception?"

"I merely saw her. Was she unsatisfactory?"

"She was very clever. I never looked pret-
tier, I am sure. The maid is a little, demure
thing, very young for such a position, and positively homely and common in appearance. But
I hardly noticed her until she dropped a letter
from her clothing. It fell just beside me, and I
saw that it was addressed to no less a personage
than my rich aunt, Miss Jane Merrick, at Elmhurst. Curious to know why a hair-dresser
should be in correspondence with Aunt Jane, I
managed to conceal the letter under my skirts
until the maid was gone. Then I put it away
until after the reception. It was sealed and
stamped, all ready for the post, but I moistened
the flap and easily opened it. Guess what I
read?"

"I've no idea," replied Mrs. Merrick.

"Here it is," continued Louise, producing a
letter and carefully unfolding it. "Listen to this,
if you please: 'Aunt Jane.' She doesn't even

say 'dear' or 'respected,' you observe. 'Your letter to me, asking me to visit you, is almost an insult after your years of silence and neglect and your refusals to assist my poor mother when she was in need. Thank God we can do without your friendship and assistance now, for my honored father, Major Gregory Doyle, is very prosperous and earns all we need. I return your check with my compliments. If you are really ill, I am sorry for you, and would go to nurse you were you not able to hire twenty nurses, each of whom would have fully as much love and far more respect for you than could ever

Your indignant niece,

Patricia Doyle.'

"What do you think of that, mamma?"

"It's very strange, Louise. This hair-dresser is your own cousin."

"So it seems. And she must be poor, or she wouldn't go out as a sort of lady's maid. I remember scolding her severely for pulling my hair at one time, and she was as meek as Moses, and never answered a word."

"She has a temper though, as this letter

AUNT JANE'S NIECES.

proves," said Mrs. Merrick; "and I admire her
for the stand she has taken."

"So do I," rejoined Louise with a laugh, "for
it removes a rival from my path. You will notice that Aunt Jane has sent her a check for the
same amount she sent me. Here it is, folded in
the letter. Probably my other cousin, the De
Graf girl, is likewise invited to Elmhurst? Aunt
Jane wanted us all, to see what we were like, and
perhaps to choose between us."

"Quite likely," said Mrs. Merrick, uneasily
watching her daughter's face.

"That being the case," continued Louise, "I
intend to enter the competition. With this child
Patricia out of the way, it will be a simple duel
with my unknown De Graf cousin for my aunt's
favor, and the excitement will be agreeable even
if I am worsted."

"There's no danger of that," said her mother,
calmly. "And the stakes are high, Louise. I've
learned that your Aunt Jane is rated as worth
a half million dollars."

"They shall be mine," said the daughter,
with assurance. "Unless, indeed, the De Graf

39

girl is most wonderfully clever. What is her name?"

"Elizabeth, if I remember rightly. But I am not sure she is yet alive, my dear. I haven't heard of the De Grafs for a dozen years."

"Anyway I shall accept my Aunt Jane's invitation, and make the acceptance as sweet as Patricia Doyle's refusal is sour. Aunt Jane will be simply furious when she gets the little hairdresser's note."

"Will you send it on?"

"Why not? It's only a question of resealing the envelope and mailing it. And it will be sure to settle Miss Doyle's chances of sharing the inheritance, for good and all."

"And the check?"

"Oh, I shall leave the check inside the envelope. It wouldn't be at all safe to cash it, you know."

"But if you took it out Jane would think the girl had kept the money, after all, and would be even more incensed against her."

"No," said Louise, after a moment's thought, "I'll not do a single act of dishonesty that could ever by any chance be traced to my door. To be cunning, to be diplomatic, to play the game of life with the best cards we can draw, is every woman's privilege. But if I can't win honestly, mater dear, I'll quit the game, for even money can't compensate a girl for the loss of her self-respect."

Mrs. Merrick cast a fleeting glance at her daughter and smiled. Perhaps the heroics of Louise did not greatly impress her.

# CHAPTER V.

## AUNT JANE.

"Lift me up, Phibbs—no, not that way! Confound your awkwardness—do you want to break my back? There! That's better. Now the pillow at my head. Oh—h. What are you biinking at, you old owl?"

"Are you better this morning, Miss Jane?" asked the attendant, with grave deference.

"No; I'm worse."

"You look brighter, Miss Jane."

"Don't be stupid, Martha Phibbs. I know how I am, better than any doctor, and I tell you I'm on my last legs."

"Anything unusual, Miss?"

"Of course. I can't be on my last legs regularly, can I?"

"I hope not, Miss."

"What do you mean by that? Are you trying to insult me, now that I'm weak and helpless? Answer me, you gibbering idiot!"

"I'm sure you'll feel better soon, Miss. Can't
I wheel you into the garden? It's a beautiful
day, and quite sunny and warm already."

"Be quick about it, then; and don't tire me
out with your eternal doddering. When a thing
has to be done, do it. That's my motto."

"Yes, Miss Jane."

Slowly and with care the old attendant
wheeled her mistress's invalid chair through the
doorway of the room, along a stately passage,
and out upon a broad piazza at the back of the
mansion. Here were extensive and carefully
tended gardens, and the balmy morning air was
redolent with the odor of flowers.

Jane Merrick sniffed the fragrance with evident enjoyment, and her sharp grey eyes sparkled as she allowed them to roam over the gor-
geous expanse of colors spread out before her.

"I'll go down, I guess, Phibbs. This may be
my last day on earth, and I'll spend an hour with

my flowers before I bid them good-bye forever."

Phibbs pulled a bell-cord, and a soft far-
away jingle was heard. Then an old man came
slowly around the corner of the house. His bare
head was quite bald. He wore a short canvas
apron and carried pruning-shears in one hand.
Without a word of greeting to his mistress or
scarce a glance at her half recumbent form, he
mounted the steps of the piazza and assisted
Phibbs to lift the chair to the ground.

"How are the roses coming on, James?"

"Poorly, Miss," he answered, and turning
his back returned to his work around the corner. If he was surly, Miss Jane seemed not to
mind it. Her glance even softened a moment as
she followed his retreating form.

But now she was revelling amongst the flowers, which she seemed to love passionately.
Phibbs wheeled her slowly along the narrow
paths between the beds, and she stopped frequently to fondle a blossom or pull away a dead
leaf or twig from a bush. The roses were magnificent, in spite of the old gardener's croaking,

44

and the sun was warm and grateful and the hum of the bees musical and sweet.

"It's hard to die and leave all this, Phibbs," said the old woman, a catch in her voice. "But it's got to be done."

"Not for a while yet, I hope, Miss Jane."

"It won't be long, Phibbs. But I must try to live until my nieces come, and I can decide which of them is most worthy to care for the old place when I am gone."

"Yes, Miss."

"I've heard from two of them, already. They jumped at the bait I held out quickly enough; but that's only natural. And the letters are very sensible ones, too. Elizabeth DeGraf says she will be glad to come, and thanks me for inviting her. Louise Merrick is glad to come, also, but hopes I am deceived about my health and that she will make me more than one visit after we become friends. A very proper feeling; but I'm not deceived, Phibbs. My end's in plain sight."

"Yes, Miss Jane."

"And somebody's got to have my money

45

and dear Elmhurst when I'm through with them. Who will it be, Phibbs?"

"I'm sure I don't know, Miss."

"Nor do I. The money's mine, and I can do what I please with it; and I'm under no obligation to anyone."

"Except Kenneth," said a soft voice behind her.

Jane Merrick gave a start at the interruption and turned red and angry as, without looking around, she answered:

"Stuff and nonsense! I know my duties and my business, Silas Watson."

"To be sure," said a little, withered man, passing around the chair and facing the old woman with an humble, deprecating air. He was clothed in black, and his smooth-shaven, deeply lined face was pleasant of expression and not without power and shrewd intelligence. The eyes, however, were concealed by heavy-rimmed spectacles, and his manner was somewhat shy and reserved. However, he did not hesitate to speak frankly to his old friend, nor minded in the least if he aroused her ire.

# AUNT JANE'S NIECES.

"No one knows better than you, dear Miss Jane, her duties and obligations; and no one performs them more religiously. But your recent acts, I confess, puzzle me. Why should you choose from a lot of inexperienced, incompetent girls a successor to Thomas Bradley's fortune, when he especially requested you in his will to look after any of his relatives, should they need assistance? Kenneth Forbes, his own nephew, was born after Tom's death, to be sure; but he is alone in the world now, an orphan, and has had no advantages to help him along in life since his mother's death eight years ago. I think Tom Bradley must have had a premonition of what was to come even though his sister was not married at the time of his death, and I am sure he would want you to help Kenneth now."

"He placed me under no obligations to leave the boy any money," snapped the old woman, white with suppressed wrath, "you know that well enough, Silas Watson, for you drew up the will."

The old gentleman slowly drew a pattern

AUNT JANE'S NIECES.

upon the gravelled walk with the end of his walking-stick.

"Yes, I drew up the will," he said, deliberately, "and I remember that he gave to you, his betrothed bride, all that he possessed—gave it gladly and lovingly, and without reserve. He was very fond of you, Miss Jane. But perhaps his conscience pricked him a bit, after all, for he added the words: 'I shall expect you to look after the welfare of my only relative, my sister, Katherine Bradley—or any of her heirs.' It appears to me, Miss Jane, that that is a distinct obligation. The boy is now sixteen and as fine a fellow as one often meets."

"Bah! An imbecile—an awkward, ill-mannered brat who is only fit for a stable-boy! I know him, Silas, and I know he'll never amount to a hill of beans. Leave *him* my money? Not if I hadn't a relative on earth!"

"You misjudge him, Jane. Kenneth is all right if you'll treat him decently. But he won't stand your abuse and I don't think the less of him for that."

"Why abuse? Haven't I given him a home

48

and an education, all because Thomas asked me to look after his relatives? And he's been rebellious and pig-headed and sullen in return for my kindness, so naturally there's little love lost between us."

"You resented your one obligation, Jane; and although you fulfilled it to the letter you did not in the spirit of Tom Bradley's request. I don't blame the boy for not liking you."

"Sir!"

"All right, Jane; fly at me if you will," said the little man, with a smile; "but I intend to tell you frankly what I think of your actions, just as long as we remain friends."

Her stern brows unbent a trifle.

"That's why we are friends, Silas; and it's useless to quarrel with you now that I'm on my last legs. A few days more will end me, I'm positive; so bear with me a little longer, my friend."

He took her withered hand in his and kissed it gently.

"You're not so very bad, Jane," said he, "and I'm almost sure you will be with us for a long

time to come.   But you're more nervous and
irritable than usual, I'll admit, and I fear this in-
vasion of your nieces won't be good for you.
Are they really coming?"

"Two of them are, I'm sure, for they've accepted my invitation," she replied.

"Here's a letter that just arrived," he said,
taking it from his pocket.   "Perhaps it contains
news from the third niece."

"My glasses, Phibbs!" cried Miss Jane,
eagerly, and the attendant started briskly for the
house to get them.

"What do you know about these girls?"
asked the old lawyer curiously.

"Nothing whatever.   I scarcely knew of their
existence until you hunted them out for me and
found they were alive.   But I'm going to know
them, and study them, and the one that's most
capable and deserving shall have my property."

Mr. Watson sighed.

"And Kenneth?" he asked.

"I'll provide an annuity for the boy, although
it's more than he deserves.   When I realized
that death was creeping upon me I felt a strange

desire to bequeath my fortune to one of my own flesh and blood. Perhaps I didn't treat my brothers and sisters generously in the old days, Silas."

"Perhaps not," he answered.

"So I'll make amends to one of their children. That is, if any one of the three nieces should prove worthy."

"I see. But if neither of the three is worthy?"

"Then I'll leave every cent to charity—except Kenneth's annuity."

The lawyer smiled.

"Let us hope," said he, "that they will prove all you desire. It would break my heart, Jane, to see Elmhurst turned into a hospital."

Phibbs arrived with the spectacles, and Jane Merrick read her letter, her face growing harder with every line she mastered. Then she crumpled the paper fiercely in both hands, and a moment later smoothed it out carefully and replaced it in the envelope.

Silas Watson had watched her silently.

"Well," said he, at last, "another acceptance?"

"No, a refusal," said she. "A refusal from the Irishman's daughter, Patricia Doyle."

"That's bad," he remarked, but in a tone of relief.

"I don't see it in that light at all," replied Miss Jane. "The girl is right. It's the sort of letter I'd have written myself, under the circumstances. I'll write again, Silas, and humble myself, and try to get her to come."

"You surprise me!" said the lawyer.

"I surprise myself," retorted the old woman, "but I mean to know more of this Patricia Doyle. Perhaps I've found a gold mine, Silas Watson!"

# CHAPTER VI.

## THE BOY.

Leaving the mistress of Elmhurst among her flowers, Silas Watson walked slowly and thoughtfully along the paths until he reached the extreme left wing of the rambling old mansion. Here, half hidden by tangled vines of climbing roses, he came to a flight of steps leading to an iron-railed balcony, and beyond this was a narrow stairway to the rooms in the upper part of the wing.

Miss Merrick, however ungenerous she might have been to others, had always maintained Elmhurst in a fairly lavish manner. There were plenty of servants to look after the house and gardens, and there were good horses in the stables. Whenever her health permitted she dined in state each evening in the great din-

53

ing-room, solitary and dignified, unless on rare occasions her one familiar, Silas Watson, occupied the seat opposite her. "The boy," as he was contemptuously called, was never permitted to enter this room. Indeed, it would be difficult to define exactly Kenneth Forbes' position at Elmhurst. He had lived there ever since his mother's death, when, a silent and unattractive lad of eight, Mr. Watson had brought him to Jane Merrick and insisted upon her providing a home for Tom Bradley's orphaned nephew.

She accepted the obligation reluctantly enough, giving the child a small room in the left wing, as far removed from her own apartments as possible, and transferring all details of his care to Misery Agnew, the old housekeeper. Misery endeavored to "do her duty" by the boy, but appreciating the scant courtesy with which he was treated by her mistress, it is not surprising the old woman regarded him merely as a dependent and left him mostly to his own devices.

Kenneth, even in his first days at Elmhurst, knew that his presence was disagreeable to Miss Jane, and as the years dragged on he grew shy and retiring, longing to break away from his unpleasant surroundings, but knowing of no other place where he would be more welcome. His only real friend was the lawyer, who neglected no opportunity to visit the boy and chat with him in his cheery manner. Mr. Watson also arranged with the son of the village curate to tutor Kenneth and prepare him for college; but either the tutor was incompetent or the pupil did not apply himself, for at twenty Kenneth Forbes was very ignorant, indeed, and seemed not to apply himself properly to his books.

He was short of stature and thin, with a sad drawn face and manners that even his staunch friend, Silas Watson, admitted were awkward and unprepossessing. What he might have been under different conditions or with different treatment, could only be imagined. Slowly climbing the stairs to the little room Kenneth inhabited, Mr. Watson was forced to conclude, with a sigh of regret, that he could not blame Miss Jane for wishing to find a more desirable heir to her estate than this graceless, sullen youth who had been thrust upon her by a thoughtless request contained in the will of her dead lover—a request that she seemed determined to fulfil literally, as it only required her to "look after" Tom's relatives and did not oblige her to leave Kenneth her property.

Yet, strange as it may seem, the old lawyer was exceedingly fond of the boy, and longed to see him the master of Elmhurst. Sometimes, when they were alone, Kenneth forgot his sense of injury and dependence, and spoke so well and with such animation that Mr. Watson was astonished, and believed that hidden underneath the mask of reserve was another entirely different personality, that in the years to come might change the entire nature of the neglected youth and win for him the respect and admiration of the world. But these fits of brightness and geniality were rare. Only the lawyer had as yet discovered them.

Today he found the boy lying listlessly upon the window-seat, an open book in his hand, but his eyes fixed dreamily upon the grove of huge elm trees that covered the distant hills.

"Morning, Ken," said he, briefly, sitting beside his young friend and taking the book in his own hand. The margins of the printed pages were fairly covered with drawings of every description. The far away trees were there and the near-by rose gardens. There was a cat spitting at an angry dog, caricatures of old Misery and James, the gardener, and of Aunt Jane and even Silas Watson himself—all so clearly depicted that the lawyer suddenly wondered if they were not clever, and an evidence of genius. But the boy turned to look at him, and the next moment seized the book from his grasp and sent it flying through the open window, uttering at the same time a rude exclamation of impatience.

The lawyer quietly lighted his pipe.

"Why did you do that, Kenneth?" he asked. "The pictures are clever enough to be preserved. I did not know you have a talent for drawing."

The boy glanced at him, but answered nothing, and the lawyer thought best not to pursue the subject. After smoking a moment in silence he remarked:

"Your aunt is failing fast." Although no

relative, Kenneth had been accustomed to speak of Jane Merrick as his aunt.

Getting neither word nor look in reply the lawyer presently continued:

"I do not think she will live much longer."

The boy stared from the window and drummed on the sill with his fingers.

"When she dies," said Mr. Watson, in a musing tone, "there will be a new mistress at Elmhurst and you will have to move out."

The boy now turned to look at him, enquiringly.

"You are twenty, and you are not ready for college. You would be of no use in the commercial world. You have not even the capacity to become a clerk. What will you do, Kenneth? Where will you go?"

The boy shrugged his shoulders.

"When will Aunt Jane die?" he asked.

"I hope she will live many days yet. She may die tomorrow."

"When she does, I'll answer your question," said the boy, roughly. "When I'm turned out of this place—which is part prison and part par-

adise—I'll do something. I don't know what,
and I won't bother about it till the time comes.
But I'll do something."

"Could you earn a living?" asked the old
lawyer.

"Perhaps not; but I'll get one. Will I be a
beggar?"

"I don't know. It depends on whether Aunt
Jane leaves you anything in her will."

"I hope she won't leave me a cent!" cried
the boy, with sudden fierceness. "I hate her,
and will be glad when she is dead and out of my
way!"

"Kenneth—Kenneth, lad!"

"I hate her!" he persisted, with blazing eyes.
"She has insulted me, scorned me, humiliated
me every moment since I have known her. I'll
be glad to have her die, and I don't want a cent
of her miserable money."

"Money," remarked the old man, knocking
the ashes from his pipe, "is very necessary to one
who is incompetent to earn his salt. And the
money she leaves you—if she really does leave

you any—won't be her's, remember, but your Uncle Tom's."

"Uncle Tom was good to my father," said the boy, softening.

"Well, Uncle Tom gave his money to Aunt Jane, whom he had expected to marry; but he asked her to care for his relatives, and she'll doubtless give you enough to live on. But the place will go to some one else, and that means you must move on."

"Who will have Elmhurst?" asked the boy.

"One of your aunt's nieces, probably. She has three, it seems, all of them young girls, and she has invited them to come here to visit her."

"Girls! Girls at Elmhurst?" cried the boy, shrinking back with a look of terror in his eyes.

"To be sure. One of the nieces, it seems, refuses to come; but there will be two of them to scramble for your aunt's affection."

"She has none," declared the boy.

"Or her money, which is the same thing. The one she likes the best will get the estate."

Kenneth smiled, and with the change of expression his face lighted wonderfully.

"Poor Aunt!" he said. "Almost I am tempted to be sorry for her. Two girls—fighting one
against the other for Elmhurst—and both fawn-
ing before a cruel and malicious old woman who
could never love anyone but herself."

"And her flowers," suggested the lawyer.

"Oh, yes; and perhaps James. Tell me, why
should she love James, who is a mere gardener,
and hate me?"

"James tends the flowers, and the flowers are
Jane Merrick's very life. Isn't that the explanation?"

"I don't know."

"The girls need not worry you, Kenneth. It
will be easy for you to keep out of their way."

"When will they come?"

"Next week, I believe."

The boy looked around helplessly, with the
air of a caged tiger.

"Perhaps they won't know I'm here," he
said.

"Perhaps not. I'll tell Misery to bring all
your meals to this room, and no one ever comes
to this end of the garden. But if they find you,

Kenneth, and scare you out of your den, run over to me, and I'll keep you safe until the girls are gone."

"Thank you, Mr. Watson," more graciously than was his wont. "It isn't that I'm afraid of girls, you know; but they may want to insult me, just as their aunt does, and I couldn't bear any more cruelty."

"I know nothing about them," said the lawyer, "so I can't vouch in any way for Aunt Jane's nieces. But they are young, and it is probable they'll be as shy and uncomfortable here at Elmhurst as you are yourself. And after all, Kenneth boy, the most important thing just now is your own future. What in the world is to become of you?"

"Oh, *that*," answered the boy, relapsing into his sullen mood; "I can't see that it matters much one way or another. Anyhow, I'll not bother my head about it until the time comes and as far as you're concerned, it's none of your business."

# CHAPTER VII.

## THE FIRST WARNING.

For a day or two Jane Merrick seemed to improve in health. Indeed, Martha Phibbs declared her mistress was better than she had been for weeks. Then, one night, the old attendant was awakened by a scream, and rushed to her mistress' side.

"What is it, ma'am?" she asked, tremblingly.

"My leg! I can't move my leg," gasped the mistress of Elmhurst. "Rub it, you old fool! Rub it till you drop, and see if you can bring back the life to it."

Martha rubbed, of course, but the task was useless. Oscar the groom was sent on horseback for the nearest doctor, who came just as day was breaking. He gave the old woman a brief examination and shook his head.

"It's the first warning,"said he; "but nothing to be frightened about. That is, for the present."

"Is it paralysis?" asked Jane Merrick.

"Yes; a slight stroke."

"But I'll have another?"

"Perhaps, in time."

"How long?"

"It may be a week—or a month—or a year. Sometimes there is never another stroke. Don't worry, ma'am. Just lie still and be comfortable."

"Huh!" grunted the old woman. But she became more composed and obeyed the doctor's instructions with unwonted meekness. Silas Watson arrived during the forenoon, and pressed her thin hand with real sympathy, for these two were friends despite the great difference in their temperaments.

"Shall I draw your will, Jane?" he asked.

"No!" she snapped. "I'm not going to die just yet, I assure you. I shall live to carry out my plans, Silas."

She did live, and grew better as the days wore on, although she never recovered the use of the paralyzed limb.

64

Each day Phibbs drew the invalid chair to the porch and old James lifted it to the garden walk, where his mistress might enjoy the flowers he so carefully and skillfully tended. They seldom spoke together, these two; yet there seemed a strange bond of sympathy between them.

At last the first of July arrived, and Oscar was dispatched to the railway station, four miles distant, to meet Miss Elizabeth De Graf, the first of the nieces to appear in answer to Jane Merrick's invitation.

Beth looked very charming and fresh in her new gown, and she greeted her aunt with a calm graciousness that would have amazed the professor to behold. She had observed carefully the grandeur and beauty of Elmhurst, as she drove through the grounds, and instantly decided the place was worth an effort to win.

"So, this is Elizabeth, is it?" asked Aunt Jane, as the girl stood before her for inspection. "You may kiss me, child."

Elizabeth advanced, striving to quell the antipathy she felt to kiss the stern featured, old woman, and touched her lips to the wrinkled forehead.

Jane Merrick laughed, a bit sneeringly, while Beth drew back, still composed, and looked at her relative enquiringly.

"Well, what do you think of me?" demanded Aunt Jane, as if embarrassed at the scrutiny she received.

"Surely, it is too early to ask me that," replied Beth, gently. "I am going to try to like you, and my first sight of my new aunt leads me to hope I shall succeed."

"Why shouldn't you like me?" cried the old woman. "Why must you try to like your mother's sister?"

Beth flushed. She had promised herself not to become angry or discomposed, whatever her aunt might say or do; but before she could control herself an indignant expression flashed across her face and Jane Merrick saw it.

"There are reasons," said Beth, slowly, "why your name is seldom mentioned in my father's family. Until your letter came I scarcely knew I possessed an aunt. It was your desire we should become better acquainted, and I am here for that purpose. I hope we shall become friends, Aunt Jane, but until then, it is better we should not discuss the past."

The woman frowned. It was not difficult for her to read the character of the child before her, and she knew intuitively that Beth was strongly prejudiced against her, but was honestly trying not to allow that prejudice to influence her. She decided to postpone further interrogations until another time.

"Your journey has tired you," she said abruptly. "I'll have Misery show you to your room."

She touched a bell beside her.

"I'm not tired, but I'll go to my room, if you please," answered Beth, who realized that she had in some way failed to make as favorable an impression as she had hoped. "When may I see you again?"

"When I send for you," snapped Aunt Jane, as the housekeeper entered. "I suppose you know I am a paralytic, and liable to die at any time?"

AUNT JANE'S NIECES.

"I am very sorry," said Beth, hesitatingly.
"You do not seem very ill."

"I'm on my last legs. I may not live an
hour. But that's none of your business, I suppose. By the way, I expect your cousin on the
afternoon train."

Beth gave a start of surprise.

"My cousin?" she asked.

"Yes, Louise Merrick."

"Oh!" said Beth, and stopped short.

"What do you mean by that?" enquired
Aunt Jane, with a smile that was rather malicious.

"I did not know I had a cousin," said the
girl. "That is," correcting herself, "I did not
know whether Louise Merrick was alive or not.
Mother has mentioned her name once or twice
in my presence; but not lately."

"Well, she's alive. Very much alive, I believe. And she's coming to visit me, while you
are here. I expect you to be friends."

"To be sure," said Beth, nevertheless discom-
fited at the news.

"We dine at seven," said Aunt Jane. "I al-

68

ways lunch in my own room, and you may do the same," and with a wave of her thin hand she dismissed the girl, who thoughtfully followed the old housekeeper through the halls.

It was not going to be an easy task to win this old woman's affection. Already she rebelled at the necessity of undertaking so distasteful a venture and wondered if she had not made a mistake in trying to curb her natural frankness, and to conciliate a creature whose very nature seemed antagonistic to her own. And this new cousin, Louise Merrick, why was she coming to Elmhurst? To compete for the prize Beth had already determined to win? In that case she must consider carefully her line of action, that no rival might deprive her of this great estate. Beth felt that she could fight savagely for an object she so much desired. Her very muscles hardened and grew tense at the thought of conflict as she walked down the corridor in the wake of old Misery the housekeeper. She had always resented the sordid life at Cloverton. She had been discontented with her lot since her earliest girlhood, and longed to escape the constant bickerings of her parents and their vain struggles to obtain enough money to "keep up appearances" and drive the wolf from the door. And here was an opportunity to win a fortune and a home beautiful enough for a royal princess. All that was necessary was to gain the esteem of a crabbed, garrulous old woman, who had doubtless but a few more weeks to live. It must be done, in one way or another; but how? How could she outwit this unknown cousin, and inspire the love of Aunt Jane?

"If there's any stuff of the right sort in my nature," decided the girl, as she entered her pretty bedchamber and threw herself into a chair, "I'll find a way to win out. One thing is certain—I'll never again have another chance at so fine a fortune, and if I fail to get it I shall deserve to live in poverty forever afterward."

Suddenly she noticed the old housekeeper standing before her and regarding her with a kindly interest. In an instant she sprang up, threw her arms around Misery and kissed her furrowed cheek.

"Thank you for being so kind," said she.

"I've never been away from home before and you must be a mother to me while I'm at Elmhurst."

Old Misery smiled and stroked the girl's glossy head.

"Bless the child!" she said, delightedly; "of course I'll be a mother to you. You'll need a bit of comforting now and then, my dear, if you're going to live with Jane Merrick."

"Is she cross?" asked Beth, softly.

"At times she's a fiend," confided the old housekeeper, in almost a whisper. "But don't you mind her tantrums, or lay 'em to heart, and you'll get along with her all right."

"Thank you," said the girl. "I'll try not to mind."

"Do you need anything else, deary?" asked Misery, with a glance around the room.

"Nothing at all, thank you."

The housekeeper nodded and softly withdrew.

"That was one brilliant move, at any rate," said Beth to herself, as she laid aside her hat and prepared to unstrap her small trunk. "I've made a friend at Elmhurst who will be of use to me; and I shall make more before long. Come as soon as you like, Cousin Louise! You'll have to be more clever than I am, if you hope to win Elmhurst."

# CHAPTER VIII.

## THE DIPLOMAT.

Aunt Jane was in her garden, enjoying the
flowers. This was her especial garden, surrounded by a high box hedge, and quite distinct
from the vast expanse of shrubbery and flower-
beds which lent so much to the beauty of the
grounds at Elmhurst. Aunt Jane knew and
loved every inch of her property. She had
watched the shrubs personally for many years,
and planned all the alterations and the construc-
tion of the flower-beds which James had so suc-
cessfully attended to. Each morning, when her
health permitted, she had inspected the green-
houses and issued her brief orders—brief because her slightest word to the old gardener in-
sured the fulfillment of her wishes. But this bit
of garden adjoining her own rooms was her

especial pride, and contained the choicest plants she had been able to secure. So, since she had been confined to her chair, the place had almost attained to the dignity of a private drawing-room, and on bright days she spent many hours here, delighting to feast her eyes with the rich coloring of the flowers and to inhale their fragrance. For however gruff Jane Merrick might be to the people with whom she came in contact, she was always tender to her beloved flowers, and her nature invariably softened when in their presence.

By and by Oscar, the groom, stepped through an opening in the hedge and touched his hat.

"Has my niece arrived?" asked his mistress, sharply.

"She's on the way, mum," the man answered, grinning. "She stopped outside the grounds to pick wild flowers, an' said I was to tell you she'd walk the rest o' the way."

"To pick wild flowers?"

"That's what she said, mum. She's that fond of 'em she couldn't resist it. I was to come

74

an' tell you this, mum; an' she'll follow me directly."

Aunt Jane stared at the man sternly, and he turned toward her an unmoved countenance. Oscar had been sent to the station to meet Louise Merrick, and drive her to Elmhurst; but this strange freak on the part of her guest set the old woman thinking what her object could be. Wild flowers were well enough in their way; but those adjoining the grounds of Elmhurst were very ordinary and unattractive, and Miss Merrick's aunt was expecting her. Perhaps—

A sudden light illumined the mystery.

"See here, Oscar; has this girl been questioning you?"

"She asked a few questions, mum."

"About me?"

"Some of 'em, if I remember right, mum, was about you."

"And you told her I was fond of flowers?"

"I may have just mentioned that you liked 'em, mum."

Aunt Jane gave a scornful snort, and the man responded in a curious way. He winked slowly and laboriously, still retaining the solemn expression on his face.

"You may go, Oscar. Have the girl's luggage placed in her room."

"Yes, mum."

He touched his hat and then withdrew, leaving Jane Merrick with a frown upon her brow that was not caused by his seeming impertinence.

Presently a slight and graceful form darted through the opening in the hedge and approached the chair wherein Jane Merrick reclined.

"Oh, my dear, dear aunt!" cried Louise. "How glad I am to see you at last, and how good of you to let me come here!" and she bent over and kissed the stern, unresponsive face with an enthusiasm delightful to behold.

"This is Louise, I suppose," said Aunt Jane, stiffly. "You are welcome to Elmhurst."

"Tell me how you are," continued the girl, kneeling beside the chair and taking the withered hands gently in her own. "Do you suffer any? And are you getting better, dear aunt, in this beautiful garden with the birds and the sunshine?"

"Get up," said the elder woman, roughly. "You're spoiling your gown."

Louise laughed gaily.

"Never mind the gown," she answered. "Tell me about yourself. I've been so anxious since your last letter."

Aunt Jane's countenance relaxed a trifle. To speak of her broken health always gave her a sort of grim satisfaction.

"I'm dying, as you can plainly see," she announced. "My days are numbered, Louise. If you stay long enough you can gather wild flowers for my coffin."

Louise flushed a trifle. A bunch of buttercups and forget-me-nots was fastened to her girdle, and she had placed a few marguerites in her hair.

"Don't laugh at these poor things!" she said, deprecatingly. "I'm so fond of flowers, and we find none growing wild in the cities, you know."

Jane Merrick looked at her reflectively.

"How old are you, Louise," she asked.

"Just seventeen, Aunt."

"I had forgotten you are so old as that. Let me see; Elizabeth cannot be more than fifteen."

"Elizabeth?"

"Elizabeth De Graf, your cousin. She arrived at Elmhurst this morning, and will be your companion while you are here."

"That is nice," said Louise.

"I hope you will be friends."

"Why not, Aunt? I haven't known much of my relations in the past, you know, so it pleases me to find an aunt and a cousin at the same time. I am sure I shall love you both. Let me fix your pillow—you do not seem comfortable. There! Isn't that better?" patting the pillow deftly. "I'm afraid you have needed more loving care than a paid attendant can give you," glancing at old Martha Phibbs, who stood some paces away, and lowering her voice that she might not be overheard. "But for a time, at least, I mean to be your nurse, and look after your wants. You should have sent for me before, Aunt Jane."

"Don't trouble yourself; Phibbs knows my ways, and does all that is required," said the invalid, rather testily. "Run away, now, Louise. The housekeeper will show you to your room. It's opposite Elizabeth's, and you will do well to make her acquaintance at once. I shall expect you both to dine with me at seven."

"Can't I stay here a little longer?" pleaded Louise. "We haven't spoken two words together, as yet, and I'm not a bit tired or anxious to go to my room. What a superb oleander this is! Is it one of your favorites, Aunt Jane?"

"Run away," repeated the woman. "I want to be alone."

The girl sighed and kissed her again, stroking the gray hair softly with her white hand.

"Very well; I'll go," she said. "But I don't intend to be treated as a strange guest, dear Aunt, for that would drive me to return home at once. You are my father's eldest sister, and I mean to make you love me, if you will give me the least chance to do so."

She looked around her, enquiringly, and Aunt Jane pointed a bony finger at the porch.

"That is the way. Phibbs will take you to

Misery, the housekeeper, and then return to me. Remember, I dine promptly at seven."

"I shall count the minutes," said Louise, and with a laugh and a graceful gesture of adieu, turned to follow Martha into the house.

Jane Merrick looked after her with a puzzled expression upon her face.

"Were she in the least sincere," she muttered, "Louise might prove a very pleasant companion. But she's not sincere; she's coddling me to win my money, and if I don't watch out she'll succeed. The girl's a born diplomat, and weighed in the balance against sincerity, diplomacy will often tip the scales. I might do worse than to leave Elmhurst to a clever woman. But I don't know Beth yet. I'll wait and see which girl is the most desirable, and give them each an equal chance."

# CHAPTER IX.

## COUSINS.

"Come in," called Beth, answering a knock at her door.

Louise entered, and with a little cry ran forward and caught Beth in her arms, kissing her in greeting.

"You must be my new cousin—Cousin Elizabeth—and I'm awfully glad to see you at last!" she said, holding the younger girl a little away, that she might examine her carefully.

Beth did not respond to the caress. She eyed her opponent sharply, for she knew well enough, even in that first moment, that they were engaged in a struggle for supremacy in Aunt Jane's affections, and that in the battles to come no quarter could be asked or expected.

So they stood at arm's length, facing one another and secretly forming an estimate each of the other's advantages and accomplishments.

"She's pretty enough, but has no style whatever," was Louise's conclusion. "Neither has she tact nor self-possession, or even a prepossessing manner. She wears her new gown in a dowdy manner and one can read her face easily. There's little danger in this quarter, I'm sure, so I may as well be friends with the poor child."

As for Beth, she saw at once that her "new cousin" was older and more experienced in the ways of the world, and therefore liable to prove a dangerous antagonist. Slender and graceful of form, attractive of feature and dainty in manner, Louise must be credited with many advantages; but against these might be weighed her evident insincerity—the volubility and gush that are so often affected to hide one's real nature, and which so shrewd and suspicious a woman as Aunt Jane could not fail to readily detect. Altogether, Beth was not greatly disturbed by her cousin's appearance, and suddenly realiz-

ing that they had been staring at one another
rather rudely, she said, pleasantly enough:

"Won't you sit down?"

"Of course; we must get acquainted," replied Louise, gaily, and perched herself cross-
legged upon the window-seat, surrounded by a
mass of cushions.

"I didn't know you were here, until an hour
ago," she continued. "But as soon as Aunt Jane
told me I ran to my room, unpacked and settled
the few traps I brought with me, and here I am—
prepared for a good long chat and to love you
just as dearly as you will let me."

"I knew you were coming, but not until this
morning," answered Beth, slowly. "Perhaps
had I known, I would not have accepted our
Aunt's invitation."

"Ah! Why not?" enquired the other, as if
in wonder.

Beth hesitated.

"Have you known Aunt Jane before today?" she asked.

"No."

"Nor I. The letter asking me to visit her

was the first I have ever received from her.
Even my mother, her own sister, does not cor-
respond with her. I was brought up to hate her
very name, as a selfish, miserly old woman. But,
since she asked me to visit her, we judged she
had softened and might wish to become friendly,
and so I accepted the invitation. I had no idea
you were also invited."

"But why should you resent my being here?"
Louise asked, smiling. "Surely, two girls will
have a better time in this lonely old place than
one could have alone. For my part, I am delighted to find you at Elmhurst."

"Thank you," said Beth. "That's a nice thing
to say, but I doubt if it's true. Don't let's beat
around the bush. I hate hypocrisy, and if we're
going to be friends let's be honest with one another from the start."

"Well?" queried Louise, evidently amused.

"It's plain to me that Aunt Jane has invited
us here to choose which one of us shall inherit
her money—and Elmhurst. She's old and feeble,
and she hasn't any other relations."

"Oh, yes, she has" corrected Louise.

"You mean Patricia Doyle?"

"Yes."

"What do you know of her?"

"Nothing at all."

"Where does she live?"

"I haven't the faintest idea."

Louise spoke as calmly as if she had not mailed Patricia's defiant letter to Aunt Jane, or discovered her cousin's identity in the little hair-dresser from Madame Borne's establishment.

"Has Aunt Jane mentioned her?" continued Beth.

"Not in my presence."

"Then we may conclude she's left out of the arrangement," said Beth, calmly. "And, as I said, Aunt Jane is likely to choose one of us to succeed her at Elmhurst. I hoped I had it all my own way, but it's evident I was mistaken. You'll fight for your chance and fight mighty hard!"

Louise laughed merrily.

"How funny!" she exclaimed, after a moment during during which Beth frowned at her

darkly. "Why, my dear cousin, I don't want
Aunt Jane's money."

"You don't?"

"Not a penny of it; nor Elmhurst; nor anything you can possibly lay claim to, my dear.
My mother and I are amply provided for, and I
am only here to find rest from my social duties
and to get acquainted with my dead father's sister. That is all."

"Oh!" said Beth, lying back in her chair with
a sigh of relief.

"So it was really a splendid idea of yours to
be frank with me at our first meeting," continued
Louise, cheerfully; "for it has led to your learning the truth, and I am sure you will never again
grieve me by suggesting that I wish to supplant
you in Aunt Jane's favor. Now tell me something
about yourself and your people. Are you poor?"

"Poor as poverty," said Beth, gloomily.
"My father teaches music, and mother scolds
him continually for not being able to earn enough
money to keep out of debt."

"Hasn't Aunt Jane helped you?"

"We've never seen a cent of her money, al-

though father has tried at times to borrow enough
to help him out of his difficulties."

"That's strange. She seems like such a dear
kindly old lady," said Louise, musingly.

"I think she's horrid," answered Beth, angrily; "but I mustn't let her know it. I even
kissed her, when she asked me to, and it sent a
shiver all down my back."

Louise laughed with genuine amusement.

"You must dissemble, Cousin Elizabeth," she
advised, "and teach our aunt to love you. For
my part, I am fond of everyone, and it delights
me to fuss around invalids and assist them. I
ought to have been a trained nurse, you know;
but of course there's no necessity of my earn-
ing a living."

"I suppose not," said Beth. Then, after a
thoughtful silence, she resumed abruptly;
"What's to prevent Aunt Jane leaving you her
property, even if you are rich, and don't need it?
You say you like to care for invalids, and I don't.
Suppose Aunt Jane prefers you to me, and wills
you all her money?"

"Why, that would be beyond my power to

AUNT JANE'S NIECES.

prevent," answered Louise, with a little yawn.
Beth's face grew hard again.

"You're deceiving me," she declared, angrily.
"Your're trying to make me think you don't
want Elmhurst, when you're as anxious to get
it as I am."

"My dear Elizabeth—by the way, that's an
awfully long name; what do they call you, Liz-
zie, or Bessie, or—"

"They call me Beth," sullenly.

"Then, my dear Beth, let me beg you not to
borrow trouble, or to doubt one who wishes to
be your friend. Elmhurst would be a perfect
bore to me. I wouldn't know what to do with
it. I couldn't live in this out-of-the-way corner
of the world, you know."

"But suppose she leaves it to you?" persisted
Beth. "You wouldn't refuse it, I imagine."

Louise seemed to meditate.

"Cousin," she said, at length, "I'll make a
bargain with you. I can't refuse to love and pet
Aunt Jane, just because she has money and my
sweet cousin Beth is anxious to inherit it. But
I'll not interfere in any way with your chances,

88

AUNT JANE'S NIECES.

and I'll promise to sing your praises to our aunt persistently. Furthermore, in case she selects me as her heir, I will agree to transfer half of the estate to you—the half that consists of Elmhurst."

"Is there much more?" asked Beth.

"I haven't any list of Aunt Jane's possessions, so I don't know. But you shall have Elmhurst, if I get it, because the place would be of no use to me."

"It's a magnificent estate," said Beth, looking at her cousin doubtfully.

"It shall be yours, dear, whatever Aunt Jane decides. See, this is a compact, and I'll seal it with a kiss."

She sprang up and, kneeling beside Beth, kissed her fervently.

"Now shall we be friends?" she asked, lightly. "Now will you abandon all those naughty suspicions and let me love you?"

Beth hesitated. The suggestion seemed preposterous. Such generosity savored of play acting, and Louise's manner was too airy to be genuine. Somehow she felt that she was being

89

laughed at by this slender, graceful girl, who was scarcely older than herself; but she was too unsophisticated to know how to resent it. Louise insisted upon warding off her enmity, or at least establishing a truce, and Beth, however suspicious and ungracious, could find no way of rejecting the overtures.

"Were I in your place," she said, "I would never promise to give up a penny of the inheritance. If I win it, I shall keep it all."

"To be sure. I should want you to, my dear."

"Then, since we have no cause to quarrel, we may as well become friends," continued Beth, her features relaxing a little their set expression.

Louise laughed again, ignoring the other's brusqueness, and was soon chatting away pleasantly upon other subjects and striving to draw Beth out of her natural reserve.

The younger girl had no power to resist such fascinations. Louise knew the big world, and talked of it with charming naivete, and Beth listened rapturously. Such a girl friend it had never been her privilege to have before, and when her suspicions were forgotten she became fairly responsive, and brightened wonderfully.

They dressed in time for dinner, and met Aunt Jane and Silas Watson, the lawyer, in the great drawing-room. The old gentleman was very attentive and courteous during the stately dinner, and did much to relieve the girls' embarrassment. Louise, indeed, seemed quite at home in her new surroundings, and chatted most vivaciously during the meal; but Aunt Jane was strangely silent, and Beth had little to say and seemed awkward and ill at ease.

The old lady retired to her own room shortly after dinner, and presently sent a servant to request Mr. Watson to join her.

"Silas," she said, when he entered, "what do you think of my nieces?"

"They are very charming girls," he answered, "although they are at an age when few girls show to good advantage. Why did you not invite Kenneth to dinner, Jane?"

"The boy?"

"Yes. They would be more at ease in the

society of a young gentleman more nearly their own age."

"Kenneth is a bear. He is constantly saying disagreeable things. In other words, he is not gentlemanly, and the girls shall have nothing to do with him."

"Very well," said the lawyer, quietly.

"Which of my nieces do you prefer?" asked the old lady, after a pause.

"I cannot say, on so short an acquaintance," he answered, with gravity. "Which do you prefer, Jane?"

"They are equally unsatisfactory," she answered. "I cannot imagine Elmhurst belonging to either, Silas." Then she added, with an abrupt change of manner: "You must go to New York for me, at once."

"Tonight?"

"No; tomorrow morning. I must see that other niece—the one who defies me and refuses to answer my second letter."

"Patricia Doyle?"

"Yes. Find her and argue with her. Tell her I am a crabbed old woman with a whim to know her, and that I shall not die happy unless she comes to Elmhurst. Bribe her, threaten her —kidnap her if necessary, Silas; but get her to Elmhurst as quickly as possible."

"I'll do my best, Jane. But why are you so anxious?"

"My time is drawing near, old friend," she replied, less harshly than usual, "and this matter of my will lies heavily on my conscience. What if I should die tonight?"

He did not answer.

"There would be a dozen heirs to fight for my money, and dear old Elmhurst would be sold to strangers," she resumed, with bitterness. "But I don't mean to cross over just yet, Silas, even if one limb is dead already. I shall hang on until I get this matter settled, and I can't settle it properly without seeing all three of my nieces. One of these is too hard, and the other too soft. I'll see what Patricia is like."

"She may prove even more undesirable," said the lawyer.

"In that case, I'll pack her back again and choose between these two. But you must fetch

93

her, Silas, that I may know just what I am doing. And you must fetch her at once!"

"I'll do the best I can, Jane," repeated the old lawyer.

# CHAPTER X.

In the harness-room above the stable sat Duncan Muir, the coachman and most important servant, with the exception of the head gardener, in Miss Merrick's establishment. Duncan, bald-headed but with white and bushy side-whiskers, was engaged in the serious business of oiling and polishing the state harness, which had not been used for many months past. But that did not matter. Thursday was the day for oiling the harness, and so on Thursday he performed the task, never daring to entrust a work so important to a subordinate.

In one corner of the little room Kenneth Forbes squatted upon a bench, with an empty pine box held carelessly in his lap. While Dun-

95

can worked the boy was busy with his pencil, but neither had spoken for at least a half hour.

Finally the aged coachman, without looking up, enquired:

"What do ye think o' 'em, Kenneth lad?"

"Think o' whom, Don?"

"The young leddies."

"What young ladies?"

"Miss Jane's nieces, as Oscar brought from the station yesterday."

The boy looked astonished, and leaned over the box in his lap eagerly.

"Tell me, Don," he said. "I was away with my gun all yesterday, and heard nothing of it."

"Why, it seems Miss Jane's invited 'em to make her a visit."

"But not yet, Don! Not so soon."

"Na'theless, they're here."

"How many, Don?"

"Two, lad. A bonny young thing came on the morning train, an' a nice, wide-awake one by the two o'clock."

"Girls?" with an accent of horror.

AUNT JANE'S NIECES.

"Young females, anyhow," said Donald, polishing a buckle briskly.

The boy glared at him fixedly.

"Will they be running about the place, Don?"

"Most likely. 'Twould be a shame to shut
them up with the poor missus this glad weather.
But why not? They'll be company for ye, Kenneth lad."

"How long will they stay?"

"Mebbe for aye. Oscar forbys one or the
ither o' 'em will own the place when Miss Jane
gi'es up the ghost."

The boy sat silent a moment, thinking upon
this speech. Then, with a cry that was almost a
scream, he dashed the box upon the floor and
flew out the door as if crazed, and Donald paused
to listen to his footsteps clattering down the
stairs.

Then the old man groaned dismally, shaking
his side-whiskers with a negative expression that
might have conveyed worlds of meaning to one
able to interpret it. But his eye fell upon the
pine box, which had rolled to his feet, and he
stooped to pick it up. Upon the smoothly planed

side was his own picture, most deftly drawn, showing him engaged in polishing the harness. Every strap and buckle was depicted with rare fidelity; there was no doubt at all of the sponge and bottle on the stool beside him, or the cloth in his hand. Even his bow spectacles rested upon the bridge of his nose at exactly the right angle, and his under lip protruded just as it had done since he was a lad.

Donald was not only deeply impressed by such an exhibition of art; he was highly gratified at being pictured, and full of wonder that the boy could do such a thing: "wi' a wee pencil an' a bit o' board!" He turned the box this way and that to admire the sketch, and finally arose and brought a hatchet, with which he carefully pried the board away from the box. Then he carried his treasure to a cupboard, where he hid it safely behind a row of tall bottles.

Meantime Kenneth had reached the stable, thrown a bridle over the head of a fine sorrel mare, and scorning to use a saddle leaped upon her back and dashed down the lane and out at the rear gate upon the old turnpike road.

His head was whirling with amazement, his heart full of indignation. Girls! Girls at Elmhurst—nieces and guests of the fierce old woman he so bitterly hated! Then, indeed, his days of peace and quiet were ended. These dreadful creatures would prowl around everywhere; they might even penetrate the shrubbery to the foot of the stairs leading to his own retired room; they would destroy his happiness and drive him mad.

For this moody, silent youth had been strangely happy in his life at Elmhurst, despite the neglect of the grim old woman who was its mistress and the fact that no one aside from Lawyer Watson seemed to care whether he lived or died.

Perhaps Donald did. Good old Don was friendly and seldom bothered him by talking. Perhaps old Misery liked him a bit, also. But these were only servants, and almost as helpless and dependent as himself.

Still, he had been happy. He began to realize it, now that these awful girls had come to disturb his peace. The thought filled him with grief and rebellion and resentment; yet there

99

was nothing he could do to alter the fact that Donald's "young females" were already here, and prepared, doubtless, to stay.

The sorrel was dashing down the road at a great pace, but the boy clung firmly to his seat and gloried in the breeze that fanned his hot cheeks. Away and away he raced until he reached the crossroads, miles away, and down this he turned and galloped as recklessly as before. The sun was hot, today, and the sorrel's flanks begun to steam and show flecks of white upon their glossy surface. He turned again to the left, entering upon a broad highway that would lead him straight home at last; but he had almost reached the little village of Elmwood, which was the railway station, before he realized his cruelty to the splendid mare he bestrode. Then indeed, he fell to a walk, patting Nora's neck affectionately and begging her to forgive him for his thoughtlessness. The mare tossed her head in derision. However she might sweat and pant, she liked the glorious pace even better than her rider.

Through the village he paced moodily, the

AUNT JANE'S NIECES.

bridle dangling loosely on the mare's neck. The people paused to look at him curiously, but he had neither word nor look for any.

He did not know one of them by name, and cared little how much they might speculate upon his peculiar position at "the big house."

Then, riding slowly up the hedge bordered road, his troubles once more assailed him, and he wondered if there was not some spot upon the broad earth to which he could fly for retirement until the girls had left Elmhurst for good.

Nora shied, and he looked up to discover that he had nearly run down a pedestrian—a stout little man with a bundle under his arm, who held up one hand as if to arrest him.

Involuntarily he drew rein, and stopped beside the traveler with a look of inquiry.

"Sorry to trouble you, sir," remarked the little man, in a cheery voice, "but I ain't just certain about my way."

"Where do you want to go?" asked the boy.

"To Jane Merrick's place. They call it Elmhurst, I guess."

"It's straight ahead," said Kenneth, as the

101

mare walked on. His questioner also started and paced beside him.

"Far from here?"

"A mile, perhaps."

"They said it was three from the village, but I guess I've come a dozen a'ready."

The boy did not reply to this. There was nothing offensive in the man's manner. He spoke with an easy familiarity that made it difficult not to respond with equal frank cordiality, and there was a shrewd expression upon his wrinkled, smooth-shaven face that stamped him a man who had seen life in many of its phases.

Kenneth, who resented the companionship of most people, seemed attracted by the man, and hesitated to gallop on and leave him.

"Know Jane Merrick?" asked the stranger.

The boy nodded.

"Like her?"

"I hate her," he said, savagely.

The man laughed, a bit uneasily.

"Then it's the same Jane as ever," he responded, with a shake of his grizzled head. "Do you know, I sort o' hoped she'd reformed, and I'd be glad to see her again. They tell me she's got money."

The boy looked at him in surprise.

"She owns Elmhurst, and has mortgages on a dozen farms around here, and property in New York, and thousands of dollars in the bank," he said. "Aunt Jane's rich."

"Aunt Jane?" echoed the man, quickly. "What's your name, lad?"

"Kenneth Forbes."

A shake of the head.

"Don't recollect any Forbeses in the family."

"She isn't really my aunt," said the boy, "and she doesn't treat me as an aunt, either; but she's my guardian, and I've always called her Aunt, rather than say Miss Merrick."

"She's never married, has she?"

"No. She was engaged to my Uncle Tom, who owned Elmhurst. He was killed in a railway accident, and then it was found he'd left her all he had."

"I see."

"So, when my parents died, Aunt Jane took

me for Uncle Tom's sake, and keeps me out of charity."

"I see." Quite soberly, this time.

The boy slid off the mare and walked beside the little man, holding the bridle over his arm. They did not speak again for some moments.

Finally the stranger asked:

"Are Jane's sisters living—Julia and Violet?"

"I don't know. But there are two of her nieces at Elmhurst."

"Ha! Who are they?"

"Girls," with bitterness. "I haven't seen them."

The stranger whistled.

"Don't like girls, I take it?"

"No; I hate them."

Another long pause. Then the boy suddenly turned questioner.

"You know Aunt—Miss Merrick, sir?"

"I used to, when we were both younger."

"Any relation, sir?"

"Just a brother, that's all."

Kenneth stopped short, and the mare stopped,

and the little man, with a whimsical smile at the boy's astonishment, also stopped.

"I didn't know she had a brother, sir—that is, living."

"She had two; but Will's dead, years ago, I'm told. I'm the other."

"John Merrick?"

"That's me. I went west a long time ago; before you were born, I guess. We don't get much news on the coast, so I sort of lost track of the folks back east, and I reckon they lost track of me, for the same reason."

"You were the tinsmith?"

"The same. Bad pennies always return, they say. I've come back to look up the family and find how many are left. Curious sort of a job, isn't it."

"I don't know. Perhaps it's natural," replied the boy, reflectively. "But I'm sorry you came to Aunt Jane first."

"Why?"

"She's in bad health—quite ill, you know—and her temper's dreadful. Perhaps she—she—"

"I know. But I haven't seen her in years;

and, after all, she's my sister. And back at the old home, where I went first, no one knew anything about what had become of the family except Jane. They kept track of her because she suddenly became rich, and a great lady, and that was a surprising thing to happen to a Merrick. We've always been a poor lot, you know."

The boy glanced at the bundle, pityingly, and the little man caught the look and smiled his sweet, cheery smile.

"My valise was too heavy to carry," he said; "so I wrapped up a few things in case Jane wanted me to stay over night. And that's why I didn't get a horse at the livery, you know. Somebody'd have to take it back again."

"I'm sure she'll ask you to stay, sir. And if she doesn't, you come out to the stable and let me know, and I'll drive you to town again. Donald—that's the coachman—is my friend, and he'll let me have the horse if I ask him."

"Thank you, lad," returned the man, gratefully. "I thought a little exercise would do me good, but this three miles has seemed like thirty to me!"

"We're here at last," said the boy, turning into the drive-way. "Seeing that you're her brother, sir, I advise you to go right up to the front door and ring the bell."

"I will," said the man.

"I always go around the back way, myself."

"I see."

The boy turned away, but in a moment halted again. His interest in Miss Jane's brother John was extraordinary.

"Another thing," he said, hesitating.

"Well?"

"You'd better not say you met me, you know. It wouldn't be a good introduction. She hates me as much as I hate her."

"Very good, my lad. I'll keep mum."

The boy nodded, and turned away to lead Nora to the stable. The man looked after him a moment, and shook his head, sadly.

"Poor boy!" he whispered.

Then he walked up to the front door and rang the bell.

# CHAPTER XI.

## THE MAD GARDENER.

"This seems to be a lazy place," said Louise, as she stood in the doorway of Beth's room to bid her good night. "I shall sleep until late in the morning, for I don't believe Aunt Jane will be on exhibition before noon."

"At home I always get up at six o'clock," answered Beth.

"Six o'clock! Good gracious! What for?"

"To study my lessons and help get the breakfast."

"Don't you keep a maid?"

"No," said Beth, rather surlily; "we have hard work to keep ourselves."

"But you must be nearly through with school by this time. I finished my education ages ago."

"Did you graduate?" asked Beth.

"No; it wasn't worth while," declared Louise, complacently. "I'm sure I know as much as most girls do, and there are more useful lessons to be learned from real life than from books."

"Good night," said Beth.

"Good night," answered the older girl, and shut the door behind her.

Beth sat for a time moodily thinking. She did not like the way in which her cousin assumed superiority over her. The difference in their ages did not account for the greater worldly wisdom Louise had acquired, and in much that she said and did Beth recognized a shrewdness and experience that made her feel humbled and, in a way, inferior to her cousin. Nor did she trust the friendship Louise expressed for her.

Somehow, nothing that the girl said seemed to ring true, and Beth already, in her mind, accused her of treachery and insincerity.

As a matter of fact, however, she failed to understand her cousin. Louise really loved to be nice to people, and to say nice things. It is true she schemed and intrigued to advance her personal welfare and position in life; but even

109

her schemes were undertaken lightly and carelessly, and if they failed the girl would be the
first to laugh at her disappointment and try to
mend her fortunes. If others stood in her way
she might not consider them at all; if she pledged
her word, it might not always be profitable to
keep it; but she liked to be on pleasant terms with
everyone, and would be amiable to the last, no
matter what happened. Comedy was her forte,
rather than tragedy. If tragedy entered her life
she would probably turn it into ridicule. Wholly
without care, whimsical and generous to a de-
gree, if it suited her mood, Louise Merrick possessed a nature capable of great things, either for
good or ill.

It was no wonder her unsophisticated country
cousin failed to comprehend her, although Beth's
intuition was not greatly at fault.

Six o'clock found Beth wide awake, as usual;
so she quietly dressed and, taking her book under her arm, started to make her way into the
gardens. Despite Louise's cynicism she had no
intention of abandoning her studies. She had
decided to fit herself for a teacher before Aunt

AUNT JANE'S NIECES.

Jane's invitation had come to her, and this am-
bition would render it necessary for her to study
hard during vacations.

If she became an heiress she would not need
to teach, but she was not at all confident of her
prospects, and the girl's practical nature prompted
her to carry out her plans until she was sure of
the future.

In the hall she met Phibbs, shuffling along as
if in pain.

"Good morning, miss," said the old servant.

Beth looked at her thoughtfully. This was
Aunt Jane's special and confidential attendant.

"Do your feet hurt you?" she asked.

"Yes, miss; in the mornin' they's awful bad.
It's being on 'em all the day, 'tendin' to Miss
Jane, you know. But after a time I gets more
used to the pain, and don't feel it. The mornin's
always the worst."

She was passing on, but Beth stopped her.

"Come into my room," she said, and led the
way.

Martha Phibbs followed reluctantly. Miss
Jane might already be awake and demanding her

111

services, and she could not imagine what the young lady wanted her for.

But she entered the room, and Beth went to a box and brought out a bottle of lotion.

"Mother has the same trouble that you complain of," she said, practically, "and here is a remedy that always gives her relief. I brought it with me in case I should take long tramps, and get sore feet."

She gently pushed the old woman into a chair, and then, to Phibbs' utter amazement, knelt down and unfastened her shoes and drew off her stockings. A moment later she was rubbing the lotion upon the poor creature's swollen feet, paying no attention to Martha's horrified protests.

"There. Now they're sure to feel better," said Beth, pulling the worn and darned stockings upon the woman's feet again. "And you must take this bottle to your room, and use it every night and morning."

"Bless your dear heart!" cried Phibbs, while tears of gratitude stood in her faded eyes. "I'm sure I feel twenty years younger, a'ready. But

AUNT JANE'S NIECES.

you shouldn't 'a' done it, miss; indeed you shouldn't."

"I'm glad to help you," said Beth, rinsing her hands at the wash stand and drying them upon a towel. "It would be cruel to let you suffer when I can ease your pain."

"But what would Miss Jane say?" wailed old Martha, throwing up her hands in dismay.

"She'll never know a thing about it. It's our secret, Martha, and I'm sure if I ever need a friend you'll do as much for me."

"I'll do anything for you, Miss Elizabeth," was the reply, as the woman took the bottle of lotion and departed.

Beth smiled.

"That was not a bad thought," she said to herself, again starting for the gardens. "I have made a firm friend and done a kindly action at the same time—and all while Cousin Louise is fast asleep."

The housekeeper let her out at the side door, after Beth had pressed her hand and kissed her good morning.

"You're looking quite bonny, my dear," said

the old woman. "Do you feel at home, at all, in this strange place?"

"Not quite, as yet," answered Beth. "But I know I have one good friend here, and that comforts me."

She found a path between high hedges, that wandered away through the grounds, and along this she strolled until she reached a rose arbor with a comfortable bench.

Here she seated herself, looking around her curiously. The place seemed little frequented, but was kept with scrupulous care. Even at this hour, a little way off could be heard the "click-click!" of hedge-shears, and Beth noted how neatly the paths were swept, and how carefully every rose on the arbor was protected.

Elmhurst was a beautiful place. Beth sighed as she wondered if it would ever be hers. Then she opened her book and began to work.

During the next hour the click of the hedge-shears drew nearer, but the girl did not notice this. In another half hour James himself came into view, intent upon his monotonous task. Gradually the motionless form of the girl and the plodding figure of the gardener drew together, until he stood but two yards distant. Then he paused, looked toward the arbor, and uttered an exclamation.

Beth looked up.

"Good morning," she said, pleasantly.

James stared at her, but made no reply save a slight inclination of his head.

"Am I in your way?" she asked.

He turned his back to her, then, and began clipping away as before. Beth sprang up and laid a hand upon his arm, arresting him. Again he turned to stare at her, and in his eyes was a look almost of fear.

She drew back.

"Why won't you speak to me?" enquired the girl, gently. "I'm a stranger at Elmhurst, but I want to be your friend. Won't you let me?"

To her amazement James threw up his hands, letting the shears clatter to the ground, and with a hoarse cry turned and fled up the path as swiftly as he could go.

Beth was really puzzled, but as she stood silently looking after the gardener she heard a soft laugh, and found old Misery beside her.

"It's just his way, Miss; don't you be scared by anything that James does," said the woman. "Why, at times he won't even speak to Miss Jane."

"He isn't dumb, is he?" asked Beth.

"Lor', no! But he's that odd an' contrary he won't talk to a soul. Never did, since the day Master Tom was killed. James was travellin' with Master Tom, you know, and there was an accident, an' the train run off'n the track an' tipped over. James wasn't hurt at all, but he dragged Master Tom out'n the wreck and sat by him until he died. Then James brought Master Tom's body back home again; but his mind seemed to have got a shock, in some way, and he never was the same afterwards. He was powerful fond of young Master Tom. But then, we all was."

"Poor man!" said Beth.

"After that," resumed Misery, "all that James would do was to look after the flowers. Miss Jane, after she came, made him the head gardener, and he's proved a rare good one, too. But James he won't even talk to Miss Jane, nor even to his old friend Lawyer Watson, who used to be Master Tom's special chum an' comrade. He does his duty, and obeys all Miss Jane's orders as faithful as can be; but he won't talk, an' we've all give up tryin' to make him."

"But why should I frighten him?" asked the girl.

"You tried to make him talk, and you're a stranger. Strangers always affect James that way. I remember when Miss Jane first came to Elmhurst he screamed at the sight of her; but when he found out that Master Tom loved her and had given her Elmhurst, James followed her around like a dog, and did everything she told him to. But breakfast is ready, Miss. I came to call you."

"Thank you," said Beth, turning to walk beside the housekeeper.

According to Aunt Jane's instructions the breakfast was served in her own room, and presently Louise, dressed in a light silk kimona, came in bearing her tray "to keep her cousin company," she laughingly announced.

"I should have slept an hour longer," she yawned, over her chocolate, "but old Misery— who seems rightly named—insisted on waking me, just that I might eat. Isn't this a funny establishment?"

"It's different from everything I'm used to," answered Beth, gravely; "but it seems very pleasant here, and everyone is most kind and attentive."

"Now I'll dress," said Louise, "and we'll take a long walk together, and see the place."

So it happened that Kenneth clattered down the road on the sorrel mare just a moment before the girls emerged from the house, and while he was riding off his indignation at their presence at Elmhurst, they were doing just what his horrified imagination had depicted—that is, penetrating to all parts of the grounds, to every nook in the spacious old gardens and even to the stables, where Beth endeavored to make a friend of old Donald the coachman.

However, the gray-whiskered Scotsman was

not to be taken by storm, even by a pretty face.
His loyalty to "the boy" induced him to be wary
in associating with these strange "young females"
and although he welcomed them to the stable
with glum civility he withheld his opinion of
them until he should know them better.

In their rambles the girls found Kenneth's
own stair, and were sitting upon it when Phibbs
came to summon Louise to attend upon Aunt
Jane.

She obeyed with alacrity, for she wished to
know more of the queer relative whose guest she
had become.

"Sit down," said Aunt Jane, very graciously,
as the girl entered.

Louise leaned over the chair, kissed her and
patted her cheek affectionately, and then shook
up the pillows to make them more comfortable.

"I want you to talk to me," announced Aunt
Jane, "and to tell me something of the city and
the society in which you live. I've been so long
dead to the world that I've lost track of people
and things."

"Let me dress your hair at the same time,"

said Louise, pleadingly. "It looks really frowsy, and I can talk while I work."

"I can't lift my left hand," said the invalid, flushing, "and Phibbs is a stupid ass."

"Never mind, I can make it look beautiful in half a jiffy," said the girl, standing behind the chair and drawing deftly the hairpins from Aunt Jane's scanty grey locks, "and you can't imagine how it pleases me to fuss over anyone."

It was surprising how meekly Aunt Jane submitted to this ordeal, but she plied the girl with many shrewd questions and Louise, busily working in a position where the old woman could not see her face, never hesitated for an answer. She knew all the recent gossip of fashionable society, and retailed it glibly. She had met this celebrity at a ball and that one at a reception, and she described them minutely, realizing that Aunt Jane would never be in a position to contradict any assertion she might choose to make.

Indeed, Aunt Jane was really startled.

"However did your mother manage to gain an entrée into society?" she asked. "Your father was a poor man and of little account. I know, for he was my own brother."

"He left us a very respectable life insurance," said Louise, demurely, "and my mother had many friends who were glad to introduce us to good society when we were able to afford such a luxury. Father died twelve years ago, you know, and for several years, while I was at school, mother lived very quietly. Then she decided it was time I made my début, but for the last season we have been rather gay, I admit."

"Are you rich?" asked Aunt Jane, sharply.

"Mercy, no!" laughed Louise, who had finished her work and now sat her aunt's feet. "But we have enough for our requirements, and that makes us feel quite independent. By the way, auntie, I want to return that check you sent me. It was awfully good and generous of you, but I didn't need it, you know, and so I want you to take it back."

She drew the slip of paper from her pocket and pressed it into Aunt Jane's hand.

"It's quite enough for you to give me this nice treat in the country," resumed the girl, calm-

ly. "The change from the city will do me a world
of good, and as I wanted to be quiet, and rest
I declined all my other invitations for the summer to accept yours. Isn't it glorious that we can
get acquainted at last? And I quite love Elmhurst, already!"

Aunt Jane was equally surprised and gratified. The return of the check for a hundred dollars was very pleasant. She had drawn a simi-
lar check for each of her three nieces, believing
that it would be necessary for her to meet their
expenses, and she had considered the expenditure
in the nature of a business transaction. But Patricia had flung one check in her face, practically,
and now Louise had voluntarily returned another,
because she did not need the money. Really,
Jane Merrick was accomplishing her purpose for
less money than she had expected, and she had
hoarded her wealth for so many years that she
disliked to spend any of it foolishly.

Louise had read her nature correctly. It had
been a little hard to return so large a check, but
the girl's policy was not to appear before Aunt
Jane as a poor relation, but rather as a young

lady fitted by social education and position to become a gracious mistress of Elmhurst. This she
believed would give her a powerful advantage
over all competitors.

Whether she was right or not in this surmise
it is certain that she rose several points in Aunt
Jane's estimation during this interview, and when
she was dismissed it was so graciously that she
told herself the money her little plot had cost had
been well expended.

Afterward Elizabeth was summoned to attend
her aunt.

"I want to be amused. Can you read aloud?"
said the invalid.

"Not very well, I'm afraid. But I'll be glad
to try," answered Beth. "What do you like?"

"Select your own book," said Aunt Jane,
pointing to a heap of volumes beside her.

The girl hesitated. Louise would doubtless
have chosen a romance, or some light tale sure
to interest for the hour, and so amuse the old
lady. But Beth erroneously judged that the aged
and infirm love sober and scholarly books, and

picked out a treatise that proved ineffably dull
and tedious.

Aunt Jane sniffed, and then smiled slyly and
proceeded to settle herself for a nap. If the girl
was a fool, let her be properly punished.

Beth read for an hour, uncertain whether her
aunt were intensely interested or really asleep.
At the end of that dreadful period old Misery
entered and aroused the sleeper without cere-
mony.

"What's the matter?" asked Aunt Jane, quer-
rulously, for she resented being disturbed.

"There's a man to see you, Miss."

"Send him about his business!"

"But—"

"I won't see him, I tell you!"

"But he says he's your brother, Miss."

"Who?"

"Your brother."

Miss Jane stared as if bewildered.

"Your brother John, Miss."

The invalid sank back upon her cushions with
a sigh of resignation.

"I thought he was dead, long ago; but if he's

alive I suppose I'll have to see him," she said. "Elizabeth, leave the room. Misery, send the man here!"

# CHAPTER XII.

## UNCLE JOHN GETS ACQUAINTED.

Beth went out to find Louise, and discovered her standing near the stables, where a boy was rubbing down the sides of a sorrel mare with wisps of straw.

"Something has happened," she said to Louise in a troubled voice.

"What?"

"A man has arrived who says he is Aunt Jane's brother."

"Impossible! Have you seen him?"

"No; he says he's Aunt Jane's brother John."

"Oh; I know. The peddler, or tinker, or something or other who disappeared years ago. But it doesn't matter."

"It may matter a good deal," said practical Beth. "Aunt Jane may leave him her money."

126

AUNT JANE'S NIECES.

"Why, he's older than she is. I've heard mother say he was the eldest of the family. Aunt Jane wont leave her money to an old man, you may be sure."

Beth felt a little reassured at this, and stood for a moment beside Louise watching the boy. Presently Oscar came to him, and after touching his hat respectfully took the mare and led her into the stable. The boy turned away, with his hands in his pockets, and strolled up a path, unaware that the two dreaded girls had been observing him.

"I wonder who that is," said Beth.

"We'll find out," returned Louise. "I took him for a stable boy, at first. But Oscar seemed to treat him as a superior."

She walked into the stable, followed by her cousin, and found the groom tying the mare.

"Who was the young man?" she asked.

"Which young man, Miss?"

"The one who has just arrived with the horse."

"Oh; that's Master Kenneth, Miss," answered Oscar, with a grin.

"Where did he come from?"

"Master Kenneth? Why, he lives here."

"At the house?"

"Yes, Miss."

"Who is he?"

"Master Tom's nephew—he as used to own Elmhurst, you know."

"Mr. Thomas Bradley?"

"The same, Miss."

"Ah. How long has Master Kenneth lived here?"

"A good many years. I can't just remember how long."

"Thank you, Oscar."

The girls walked away, and when they were alone Louise remarked:

"Here is a more surprising discovery than Uncle John, Beth. The boy has a better right than any of us to inherit Elmhurst."

"Then why did Aunt Jane send for us?"

"It's a mystery, dear. Let us try to solve it."

"Come; we'll ask the housekeeper," said Beth. "I'm sure old Misery will tell us all we want to know."

AUNT JANE'S NIECES.

So they returned to the house and, with little
difficulty, found the old housekeeper.

"Master Kenneth?" she exclaimed. "Why,
he's just Master Tom's nephew, that's all."

"Is this his home?" asked Beth.

"All the home he's got, my dear. His father
and mother are both dead, and Miss Jane took
him to care for just because she thought Master
Tom would 'a' liked it."

"Is she fond of him?" enquired Louise.

"Fond of the boy? Why, Miss Jane just
hates him, for a fact. She won't even see him,
or have him near her. So he keeps to his little
room in the left wing, and eats and sleeps there."

"It's strange," remarked Beth, thoughtfully.
"Isn't he a nice boy?"

"We're all very fond of Master Kenneth," replied the housekeeper, simply. "But I'll admit
he's a queer lad, and has a bad temper. It may
be due to his lack of bringin' up, you know; for
he just runs wild, and old Mr. Chase, who comes
from the village to tutor him, is a poor lot, and
lets the boy do as he pleases. For that reason he
won't study, and he won't work, and I'm sure I

129

don't know whatever will become of him, when Miss Jane dies."

"Thank you," said Beth, much relieved, and the girls walked away with lighter hearts.

"There's no danger in that quarter, after all," said Louise, gaily. "The boy is a mere hanger-on. You see, Aunt Jane's old sweetheart, Thomas Bradley, left everything to her when he died, and she can do as she likes with it."

After luncheon, which they ate alone and un-attended save by the maid Susan, who was old Misery's daughter, the girls walked away to the rose arbor, where Beth declared they could read or sew quite undisturbed.

But sitting upon the bench they found a little old man, his legs extended, his hands thrust deep into his pockets, and a look of calm meditation upon his round and placid face. Between his teeth was a black brier pipe, which he puffed lazily.

Beth was for drawing back, but Louise took her arm and drew her forward.

"Isn't this Uncle John?" she asked.

The little man turned his eyes upon them,

withdrew his hands from his pockets and his pipe from his mouth, and then bowed profoundly.

"If you are my nieces, then I am Uncle John," he said, affably. "Sit down, my dears, and let us get acquainted."

Louise smiled, and her rapid survey took in the man's crumpled and somewhat soiled shirt-front, the frayed black necktie that seemed to have done years of faithful service, and the thick and dusty cow-hide boots. His clothing was old and much worn, and the thought crossed her mind that Oscar the groom was far neater in appearance than this newly-found relative.

Beth merely noticed that Uncle John was neither dignified nor imposing in appearance. She sat down beside him—leaving a wide space between them—with a feeling of disappointment that he was "like all the rest of the Merricks."

"You have just arrived, we hear," remarked Louise.

"Yes. Walked up from the station this fore-noon," said Uncle John. "Come to see Jane, you know, but hadn't any idea I'd find two nieces.

## AUNT JANE'S NIECES.

Hadn't any idea I possessed two nieces, to be honest about it."

"I believe you have three," said Louise, in an amused tone.

"Three? Who's the other?"

"Why, Patricia Doyle."

"Doyle? Doyle? Don't remember the name."

"I believe your sister Violet married a man named Doyle."

"So she did. Captain Doyle—or Major Doyle —or some such fellow. But what is your name?"

"I am Louise Merrick, your brother Will's daughter."

"Oh! And you?" turning to Beth.

"My mother was Julia Merrick," said Beth, not very graciously. "She married Professor De Graf. I am Elizabeth De Graf."

"Yes, yes," observed Uncle John, nodding his head. "I remember Julia very well, as a girl. She used to put on a lot of airs, and jaw father because he wouldn't have the old top-buggy painted every spring. Same now as ever, I s'pose?"

Beth did not reply.

"And Will's dead, and out of his troubles, I
hope," continued Uncle John, reflectively. "He
wrote me once that his wife had nearly driven
him crazy. Perhaps she murdered him in his
sleep—eh, Louise?"

"Sir," said Louise, much offended, "you are
speaking of my mother."

"Ah, yes. It's the same one your father
spoke of," he answered, unmoved. "But that's
neither here nor there. The fact is, I've found
two nieces," looking shrewdly from one face into
the other, "and I seem to be in luck, for you're
quite pretty and ladylike, my dears."

"Thank you," said Louise, rather coldly.
"You're a competent judge, sir, I suppose."

"Tolerable," he responded, with a chuckle.
"So good a judge that I've kep' single all my
life."

"Where did you come from?" asked the girl.

"From out on the coast," tossing his grizzled head toward the west.

"What brought you back here, after all these
years?"

AUNT JANE'S NIECES.

"Family affection, I guess. Wanted to find
out what folks yet belonged to me."

An awkward silence followed this, during
which Uncle John relighted his pipe and Beth sat
in moody silence. Louise drew a pattern in the
gravel with the end of her parasol. This new
uncle, she reflected, might become an intolerable
bore, if she encouraged his frank familiarity.

"Now that you are here," she said, presently,
"what are you going to do?"

"Nothing, my dear."

"Have you any money?"

He looked at her with a droll expression.

"Might have expected that question, my
dear," said he; "but it's rather hard to answer.
ᵀf I say no, you'll be afraid I'll want to borrow a
little spendin' money, now an' then; and if I say
yes, you'll take me for a Rockyfeller."

"Not exactly," smiled Louise.

"Well, then, if I figure close I won't have to
borrow," he responded, gravely. "And here's
Jane, my sister, just rolling in wealth that she
don't know what to do with. And she's invited

me to stay a while. So let's call the money question settled, my dear."

Another silence ensued. Louise had satisfied her curiosity concerning her new uncle, and Beth had never had any. There was nothing more to say, and as Uncle John showed no intention of abandoning the arbored seat, it was evident they must go themselves. Louise was about to rise when the man remarked:

"Jane won't last long".

"You think not?" she asked.

"She says she's half dead a'ready, and I believe it. It's about time, you know. She's let her temper and restless disposition wear her out. Pretty soon she'll blow out, like a candle. All that worries her is to keep alive until she can decide who to leave her money to. That's why you're here, I s'pose, my dears. How do you like being on exhibition, an' goin' through your paces, like a bunch o' trotting hosses, to see which is worth the most?"

"Uncle John," said Beth, "I had hoped I would like you. But if you are going to be so

very disagreeable, I'll have nothing more to do
with you!"

With this she arose and marched up the
path, vastly indignant, and Louise marched beside her. At the bend in the walk they glanced
back, and saw Uncle John sitting upon the bench
all doubled up and shaking with silent laughter.

"He's a queer old man," said Beth, flushing;
"but he's impudent and half a fool."

"Don't judge hastily, Beth," replied Louise,
reflectively. "I can't make up my mind, just yet,
whether Uncle John is a fool or not."

"Anyhow," snapped Beth, "he's laughing at
us."

"And that," said her cousin, softly, "is the
strongest evidence of his sanity. Beth, my love,
Aunt Jane has placed us in a most ridiculous position."

That evening at dinner they met Uncle John
again, seated opposite Aunt Jane in the great
dining hall. The mistress of Elmhurst always
dressed for this meal and tonight she wore a
rich black silk and had her invalid chair wheeled
to her place at the head of the table. Uncle John

had simply changed his old black necktie for a
soiled white one. Otherwise his apparel was the
same as before, and his stubby gray hair was in a
sad state of disarray. But his round face wore
a cheerful smile, nevertheless, and Aunt Jane
seemed not to observe anything *outre* in her
brother's appearance. And so the meal passed
pleasantly enough.

After it was finished Uncle John strolled into
the garden to smoke his pipe under the stars and
Louise sang a few songs for Aunt Jane in the
dimly-lit drawing room. Beth, who was a music
teacher's daughter, could not sing at all.

It was some time later when John Merrick
came to his sister's room to bid her good night.

"Well," she asked him, "what do you think
of the girls?"

"My nieces?"

"Yes."

"During my lifetime," said the old man, "I've
always noticed that girls are just girls—and nothing more. Jane, your sex is a puzzle that ain't
worth the trouble solving. You're all alike, and
what little I've seen of my nieces convinces me

AUNT JANE'S NIECES.

they're regulation females—no better nor worse than their kind."

"Louise seems a capable girl," declared Aunt Jane, musingly. "I didn't care much for her, at first; but she improves on acquaintance. She has been well trained by her mother, and is very lady-like and agreeable."

"She's smarter than the other one, but not so honest," said Uncle John.

"Beth has no tact at all," replied Aunt Jane. "But then, she's younger than Louise."

"If you're trying to figure out what they are, and what they are not," returned the man, "you've got a hard job on your hands, Jane, and like as not you'll make a mistake in the end. Where's the other niece? Aren't there three of them?"

"Yes. The other's coming. Silas Watson, my lawyer, has just telegraphed from New York that he's bringing Patricia back with him."

"Had to send for her, eh?"

"Yes. She's Irish, and if I remember rightly her father is a disgraceful old reprobate, who caused poor Violet no end of worry. The girl may be like him, for she wrote me a dreadful

138

letter, scolding me because I hadn't kept her parents supplied with money, and refusing to become my guest."

"But she's changed her mind?"

"I sent Watson after her, and he's bringing her. I wanted to see what the girl is like."

Uncle John whistled a few bars of an ancient tune.

"My advice is," he said, finally, "to let 'em draw cuts for Elmhurst. If you want to leave your money to the best o' the lot, you're as sure of striking it right that way as any other."

"Nonsense!" said Jane Merrick, sharply. "I don't want to leave my money to the best of the lot."

"No?"

"By no means. I want to leave it to the one I prefer—whether she's the best or not."

"I see. Jane, I'll repeat my former observation. Your sex is a puzzle that isn't worth solving. Good night, old girl."

"Good night, John."

# CHAPTER XIII.

## THE OTHER NIECE.

Patricia sat down opposite her Aunt Jane. She still wore her hat and the gray wrap.

"Well, here I am," she exclaimed, with a laugh; "but whether I ought to be here or not I have my doubts."

Aunt Jane surveyed her critically.

"You're a queer little thing," she said, bluntly. "I wonder why I took so much trouble to get you."

"So do I," returned Patsy, her eyes twinkling. "You'll probably be sorry for it."

Lawyer Watson, who had remained standing, now broke in nervously.

"I explained to Miss Doyle," said he, "that you were ill, and wanted to see her. And she

140

kindly consented to come to Elmhurst for a **few** days."

"You see," said Patsy, "I'd just got Daddy away on his vacation, to visit his old colonel. I've wanted him to go this three years back, but he couldn't afford it until I got a raise this Spring. He'll have a glorious old time with the colonel, and they'll fish and hunt and drink whiskey all day, and fight the war all over again every evening. So I was quite by myself when Mr. Watson came to me and wouldn't take no for his answer."

"Why did you object to come here?" asked Aunt Jane.

"Well, I didn't know you; and I didn't especially want to know you. Not that I bear grudges, understand, although you've been little of a friend to my folks these past years. But you are rich and proud—and I suspect you're a little cross, Aunt Jane—while we are poor and proud and like to live our lives in our own way."

"Are you a working girl?" enquired Miss Merrick.

"Surely," said Patsy, "and drawing a big

lump of salary every Saturday night. I'm a hair-dresser, you know—and by the way, Aunt Jane, it puzzles me to find a certain kink in your hair that I thought I'd invented myself."

"Louise dressed my hair this way," said Miss Merrick, a bit stiffly.

"Your maid?"

"My niece, Louise Merrick."

Patsy whistled, and then clapped her hand over her mouth and looked grave.

"Is she here?" she asked, a moment later.

"Yes, and your other cousin, Elizabeth De Graf, is here also."

"That's just the trouble," cried Patsy, energetically. "That's why I didn't want to come, you know."

"I don't understand you, Patricia."

"Why, it's as plain as the nose on your face, even if I hadn't pumped Mr. Watson until I got the truth out of him. You want us girls here just to compare us with each other, and pick out the one you like best."

"Well?"

## AUNT JANE'S NIECES.

"The others you'll throw over, and the favorite will get your money."

"Haven't I a right to do that?" asked the invalid, in an amazed tone.

"Perhaps you have. But we may as well understand each other right now, Aunt Jane. I won't touch a penny of your money, under any circumstances."

"I don't think you will, Patricia."

The girl laughed, with a joyous, infectious merriment that was hard to resist.

"Stick to that, aunt, and there's no reason we shouldn't be friends," she said, pleasantly. "I don't mind coming to see you, for it will give me a bit of a rest and the country is beautiful just now. More than that, I believe I shall like you. You've had your own way a long time, and you've grown crochetty and harsh and disagreeable; but there are good lines around your mouth and eyes, and your nature's liable to soften and get sunny again. I'm sure I hope so. So, if you'd like me to stay a few days, I'll take off my things and make myself at home. But I'm out of the race for your money, and I'll

143

pay my way from now on just as I have always done."

Silas Watson watched Aunt Jane's face during this speech with an anxious and half-frightened expression upon his own. No one but himself had ever dared to talk to Jane Merrick as plainly as this before, and he wondered how she would accept such frankness from a young girl.

But Patricia's manner was not at all offensive. Her big eyes were as frank as her words, but they glistened with kindliness and good nature, and it was evident the girl had no doubt at all of her aunt's reply, for she straightway begun to take off her hat.

The invalid had kept her eyes sternly fastened upon her young niece ever since the beginning of the interview. Now she reached out a hand and touched her bell.

"Misery," she said to the old housekeeper, "show my niece, Miss Patricia, to the rose chamber. And see that she is made comfortable."

"Thank you," said Patsy, jumping up to go.

"Make yourself perfectly free of the place," continued Aunt Jane, in an even tone, turning

to Patricia, "and have as good a time as you can.
I'm afraid it's rather stupid here for girls, but
that can't be helped. Stay as long as you please,
and go home whenever you like; but while you
are here, if you ever feel like chatting with a
harsh and disagreeable old woman, come to me
at any time and you will be welcome."

Patsy, standing before her, looked down into
her worn face with a pitying expression.

"Ah! I've been cruel to you," she exclaimed,
impulsively, "and I didn't mean to hurt you at
all, Aunt Jane. You must forgive me. It's
just my blunt Irish way, you see; but if I hadn't
been drawn to you from the first I wouldn't have
said a word—good or bad!"

"Go now," replied Aunt Jane, turning in her
chair rather wearily. "But come to me again
whenever you like."

Patsy nodded, and followed the housekeeper
to the rose chamber—the prettiest room old Elmhurst possessed, with broad windows opening directly upon the finest part of the garden.

Lawyer Watson sat opposite his old friend
for some moments in thoughtful silence.

"The child is impossible," he said, at last.

"You think so?" she enquired, moodily.

"Absolutely. Either of the others would make a better Lady of Elmhurst. Yet I like the little thing, I confess. She quite won my old heart after I had known her for five minutes. But money would ruin her. She's a child of the people, and ought not to be raised from her proper level. Jane, Jane—you're making a grave mistake in all this. Why don't you do the only right thing in your power, and leave Elmhurst to Kenneth?"

"You bore me, Silas," she answered, coldly. "The boy is the most impossible of all."

It was the old protest and the old reply. He had hardly expected anything different.

After a period of thought he asked:

"What is this I hear about John Merrick having returned from the West?"

"He came yesterday. It was a great surprise to me."

"I never knew this brother, I believe."

"No; he had gone away before I became acquainted with either you or Tom."

# AUNT JANE'S NIECES.

"What sort of a man is he?"

"Honest and simple, hard-headed and experienced."

"Is he independent?"

"I believe so; he has never mentioned his affairs to me. But he has worked hard all his life, he says, and now means to end his days peacefully. John is not especially refined in his manner, nor did he have much of an education; but he seems to be a good deal of a man, for all that. I am very glad he appeared at Elmhurst just at this time."

"You had believed him dead?"

"Yes. He had passed out of my life completely, and I never knew what became of him."

"He must be an eccentric person," said Mr. Watson, with a smile.

"He is," she acknowledged. "But blood is thicker than water, Silas, and I'm glad brother John is here at last."

A little later the lawyer left her and picked his way through the gardens until he came to Kenneth's wing and the stair that led to his room. Here he paused a moment, finding himself surrounded by a profound stillness, broken only by the chirping of the birds in the shrubbery. Perhaps Kenneth was not in. He half decided to retrace his steps, but finally mounted the stair softly and stood within the doorway of the room.

The boy and a little stout man were playing chess at a table, and both were in a deep study of the game. The boy's back was toward him, but the man observed the newcomer and gave a nod. Then he dropped his eyes again to the table.

Kenneth was frowning sullenly.

"You're bound to lose the pawn, whichever way you play," said the little man quietly.

The boy gave an angry cry, and thrust the table from him, sending the chess-men clattering into a corner. Instantly the little man leaned over and grasped the boy by the collar, and with a sudden jerk landed him across his own fat knees. Then, while the prisoner screamed and struggled, the man brought his hand down with a slap that echoed throughout the room, and con-

148

AUNT JANE'S NIECES.

tinued the operation until Master Kenneth had received a sound spanking.

Then he let the boy slip to the floor, from whence he arose slowly and backed toward the door, scowling and muttering angrily.

"You broke the bargain, and I kept my word," said Uncle John, calmly taking his pipe from his pocket and filling it. "The compact was that if you raised a rough-house, like you did yesterday, and got unruly, that I'd give you a good thrashing. Now, wasn't it?"

"Yes," acknowledged the boy.

"Well, that blamed temper o' your'n got away with you again, and you're well spanked for not heading it off. Pick up the board, Ken, my lad, and let's try it again."

The boy hesitated. Then he looked around and saw Lawyer Watson, who had stood motionless by the doorway, and with a cry that was half a sob Kenneth threw himself into his old friend's arms and burst into a flood of tears.

Uncle John struck a match, and lighted his pipe.

"A bargain's a bargain," he observed, composedly.

"He whipped me!" sobbed the boy. "He whipped me like a child."

"Your own fault," said Uncle John. "You wanted me to play a game with you, and I agreed, providin' you behaved yourself. And you didn't. Now, look here. Do you blame me any?"

"No," said the boy.

"No harm's done, is there?"

"No."

"Then stop blubberin', and introduce me to your friend," continued Uncle John. "Name's Watson, ain't it."

"Silas Watson, sir, at your service," said the lawyer, smiling. "And this must be John Merrick, who I understand has arrived at Elmhurst during my absence."

"Exactly," said Uncle John, and the two men shook hands cordially.

"Glad to welcome you to Elmhurst, sir," continued the lawyer. "I've known it ever since I was a boy, when it belonged to my dear friend

Thomas Bradley. And I hope you'll love it as much as I do, when you know it better."

"Bradley must have been a fool to give this place to Jane," said Uncle John, reflectively.

"He was in love, sir," observed the other, and they both smiled. Then the lawyer turned to Kenneth. "How are things going?" he asked. "Have the girls bothered you much, as yet?"

"No," said the boy. "I keep out of their way."

"That's a good idea. By the bye, sir," turning to John Merrick. "I've just brought you a new niece."

"Patricia?"

"She prefers to be called Patsy. A queer little thing; half Irish, you know."

"And half Merrick. That's an odd combination, but the Irish may be able to stand it," said Uncle John. "These nieces are more than I bargained for. I came to see one relative, and find three more—and all women!"

"I think you'll like Patsy, anyhow. And so will you, Kenneth."

The boy gave an indignant roar.

"I hate all girls!" he said.

"You won't hate this one. She's as wild and impulsive as you are, but better natured. She'll make a good comrade, although she may box your ears once in a while."

The boy turned away sulkily, and began picking up the scattered chess-men. The two men walked down the stair and strolled together through the garden.

"A strange boy," said Uncle John, presently.

"I'm glad to see you've made friends with him," replied the lawyer, earnestly. "Until now he has had no one to befriend him but me, and at times he's so unmanageable that it worries me dreadfully."

"There's considerable character about the lad," said John Merrick; "but he's been spoiled and allowed to grow up wild, like a weed. He's got it in him to make a criminal or a gentleman, whichever way his nature happens to develop."

"He ought to go to a military school," replied Lawyer Watson. "Proper training would make a man of Kenneth; but I can't induce Jane to spend the money on him. She gives him food and clothing and lodging—all of the simplest description—but there her generosity ends. With thousands of dollars lying idle, she won't assist the only nephew of Tom Bradley to secure a proper education."

"Jane's queer, too," said that lady's brother, with a sigh. "In fact, Mr. Watson, it's a queer world, and the longer I live in it the queerer I find it. Once I thought it would be a good idea to regulate things myself, and run the world as it ought to be run; but I gave it up long ago. The world's a stage, they say; but the show ain't always amusing, by a long chalk, and sometimes I wish I didn't have a reserved seat."

# CHAPTER XIV.

## KENNETH IS FRIGHTENED.

Lawyer Watson, unable to direct events at Elmhurst, became a silent spectator of the little comedy being enacted there, and never regretted that, as Uncle John expressed it, he "had a reserved seat at the show."

Jane Merrick, formerly the most imperious and irascible of women, had become wonderfully reserved since the arrival of her nieces, and was evidently making a sincere effort to study their diverse characters. Day by day the invalid's health was failing visibly. She had no more strokes of paralysis, but her left limb did not recover, and the numbness was gradually creeping upward toward her heart.

Perhaps the old woman appreciated this more fully than anyone else. At any event, she became more gentle toward Phibbs and Misery, who mostly attended her, and showed as much consideration as possible for her nieces and her brother. Silas Watson she kept constantly by her side. He was her oldest and most trusted friend, and the only differences they had ever had were over the boy Kenneth, whom she stubbornly refused to favor.

Uncle John speedily became an established fixture at the place. The servants grew accustomed to seeing him wander aimlessly about the grounds, his pipe always in his mouth, his hands usually in his pockets. He had a pleasant word always for Donald or Oscar or James, but was not prone to long conversations. Every evening, when he appeared at dinner, he wore his soiled white tie; at other times the black one was always in evidence; but other than this his dress underwent no change. Even Kenneth came to wonder what the bundle had contained that Uncle John brought under his arm to Elmhurst.

The little man seemed from the first much attracted by his three nieces. Notwithstanding Louise's constant snubs and Beth's haughty silence he was sure to meet them when they strolled out and try to engage them in conversation. It was hard to resist his simple good nature, and the girls came in time to accept him as an inevitable companion, and Louise mischievously poked fun at him while Beth conscientiously corrected him in his speech and endeavored to improve his manners. All this seemed very gratifying to Uncle John. He thanked Beth very humbly for her kind attention, and laughed with Louise when she ridiculed his pudgy, round form and wondered if his bristly gray hair wouldn't make a good scrubbing brush.

Patsy didn't get along very well with her cousins. From the first, when Louise recognized her, with well assumed surprise, as "the girl who had been sent to dress her hair," Patricia declared that their stations in life were entirely different.

"There's no use of our getting mixed up, just because we're cousins and all visiting Aunt Jane," she said. "One of you will get her money, for I've told her I wouldn't touch a penny of it, and she has told me I wouldn't get the chance. So one of you will be a great lady, while I shall always earn my own living. I'll not stay long, anyhow; so just forget I'm here, and I'll amuse myself and try not to bother you."

Both Beth and Louise considered this very sensible, and took Patricia at her word. Moreover, Phibbs had related to Beth, whose devoted adherent she was, all of the conversation between Aunt Jane and Patricia, from which the girls learned they had nothing to fear from their cousin's interference. So they let her go her way, and the three only met at the state dinners, which Aunt Jane still attended, in spite of her growing weakness.

Old Silas Watson, interested as he was in the result, found it hard to decide, after ten days, which of her nieces Jane Merrick most favored. Personally he preferred that Beth should inherit, and frankly told his old friend that the girl would make the best mistress of Elmhurst. Moreover, all the servants sang Beth's praises, from Misery and Phibbs down to Oscar and Susan. Of course James the gardener favored no one, as the numerous strangers at Elmhurst kept him in a constant state of irritation, and his malady seemed even worse than usual. He avoided everyone but his mistress, and although his work was now often neglected Miss Merrick made no complaint. James' peculiarities were well understood and aroused nothing but sympathy.

Louise, however, had played her cards so well that all Beth's friends were powerless to eject the elder girl from Aunt Jane's esteem. Louise had not only returned the check to her aunt, but she came often to sit beside her and cheer her with a budget of new social gossip, and no one could arrange the pillows so comfortably or stroke the tired head so gently as Louise. And then, she was observing, and called Aunt Jane's attention to several ways of curtailing the household expenditures, which the woman's illness had forced her to neglect.

So Miss Merrick asked Louise to look over the weekly accounts, and in this way came to depend upon her almost as much as she did upon Lawyer Watson.

As for Patsy, she made no attempt whatever

to conciliate her aunt, who seldom mentioned her name to the others but always brightened visibly when the girl came into her presence with her cheery speeches and merry laughter. She never stayed long, but came and went, like a streak of sunshine, whenever the fancy seized her; and Silas Watson, shrewdly looking on, saw a new light in Jane's eyes as she looked after her wayward, irresponsible niece, and wondered if the bargain between them, regarding the money, would really hold good.

It was all an incomprehensible problem, this matter of the inheritance, and although the lawyer expected daily to be asked to draw up Jane Merrick's will, and had, indeed, prepared several forms, to be used in case of emergency, no word had yet passed her lips regarding her intentions.

Kenneth's life, during this period, was one of genuine misery. It seemed to his morbid fancy that whatever path he might take, he was sure of running upon one or more of those detestable girls who were visiting at Elmhurst. Even in Donald's harness-room he was not secure from interruption, for little Patsy was frequently perched upon the bench there, watching with serious eyes old Donald's motions, and laughing joyously when in his embarrassment he overturned a can of oil or buckled the wrong straps together.

Worse than all, this trying creature would saddle Nora, the sorrel mare, and dash away through the lanes like a tom-boy, leaving him only old Sam to ride—for Donald would allow no one to use the coach horses. Sam was tall and boney, and had an unpleasant gait, so that the boy felt he was thoroughly justified in hating the girl who so frequently interfered with his whims.

Louise was at first quite interested in Kenneth, and resolved to force him to talk and become more sociable.

She caught him in a little summer-house one morning, from whence, there being but one entrance, he could not escape, and at once entered into conversation.

"Ah, you are Kenneth Forbes, I suppose," she began, pleasantly. "I am very glad to make

AUNT JANE'S NIECES.

your acquaintance. I am Louise Merrick, Miss Merrick's niece, and have come to visit her."

The boy shrank back as far as possible, staring her full in the face, but made no reply.

"You needn't be afraid of me," continued Louise. "I'm very fond of boys, and you must be nearly my own age."

Still no reply.

"I suppose you don't know much of girls and are rather shy," she persisted. "But I want to be friendly and I hope you'll let me. There's so much about this interesting old place that you can tell me, having lived here so many years. Come, I'll sit beside you on this bench, and we'll have a good talk together."

"Go away!" cried the boy, hoarsely, raising his hands as if to ward off her approach.

Louise looked surprised and pained.

"Why, we are almost cousins," she said. "Cannot we become friends and comrades?"

With a sudden bound he dashed her aside, so rudely that she almost fell, and an instant later he had left the summer house and disappeared among the hedges.

161

Louise laughed at her own discomfiture and gave up the attempt to make the boy's acquaintance.

"He's a regular savage," she told Beth, afterward, "and a little crazy, too, I suspect."

"Never mind," said Beth, philosophically. "He's only a boy, and doesn't amount to anything, anyway. After Aunt Jane dies he will probably go somewhere else to live. Don't let us bother about him."

Kenneth's one persistent friend was Uncle John. He came every day to the boy's room to play chess with him, and after that one day's punishment, which, singularly enough, Kenneth in no way resented, they got along very nicely together. Uncle John was a shrewd player of the difficult game, but the boy was quick as a flash to see an advantage and use it against his opponent; so neither was ever sure of winning and the interest in the game was constantly maintained. At evening also the little man often came to sit on the stair outside the boy's room and smoke his pipe, and frequently they would sit beneath the stars, absorbed in thought and without exchanging a single word.

Unfortunately, Louise and Beth soon discovered the boy's secluded retreat, and loved to torment him by entering his own bit of garden and even ascending the stairs to his little room. He could easily escape them by running through the numerous upper halls of the mansion; but here he was liable to meet others, and his especial dread was encountering old Miss Merrick. So he conceived a plan for avoiding the girls in another way.

In the hallway of the left wing, near his door, was a small ladder leading to the second story roof, and a dozen feet from the edge of the roof stood an old oak tree, on the further side of a tall hedge. Kenneth managed to carry a plank to the roof, where, after several attempts, he succeeded in dropping one end into a crotch of the oak, thus connecting the edge of the roof with the tree by means of the narrow plank. After this, at first sight of the girls in his end of the garden, he fled to the roof, ran across the improvised bridge, "shinned" down the tree and, hidden by the hedge, made good his escape.

The girls discovered this plan, and were wicked enough to surprise the boy often and force him to cross the dizzy plank to the tree. Having frightened him away they would laugh and stroll on, highly amused at the evident fear they aroused in the only boy about the place.

Patricia, who was not in the other girls' secret, knew nothing of this little comedy and really disturbed Kenneth least of the three. But he seemed to avoid her as much as he did the others.

She sooned learned from Oscar that the boy loved to ride as well as she did, and once or twice she met him on a lonely road perched on top of big Sam. This led her to suspect she had thoughtlessly deprived him of his regular mount. So one morning she said to the groom:

"Doesn't Kenneth usually ride Nora?"

"Yes, Miss," answered the man.

"Then I'd better take Sam this morning," she decided.

But the groom demurred.

"You won't like Sam, Miss," he said, "and he gets ugly at times and acts bad. Master Kenneth won't use Nora today, I'm sure."

She hesitated.

"I think I'll ask him," said she, after a moment, and turned away into the garden, anxious to have this plausible opportunity to speak to the lonely boy.

# CHAPTER XV.

## PATSY MEETS WITH AN ACCIDENT.

"Get out of here!" shouted the boy, angrily, as Patsy appeared at the foot of his stair.

"I won't!" she answered indignantly. "I've come to speak to you about the mare, and you'll just treat me decently or I'll know the reason why!"

But he didn't wait to hear this explanation. He saw her advancing up the stairs, and fled in his usual hasty manner to the hall and up the ladder to the roof.

Patsy stepped back into the garden, vexed at his flight, and the next instant she saw him appear upon the sloping roof and start to run down the plank.

Even as she looked the boy slipped, fell headlong, and slid swiftly downward. In a moment he was over the edge, clutching wildly at the plank, which was a foot or more beyond his reach. Headforemost he dove into space, but the clutching hand found something at last—the projecting hook of an old eaves-trough that had long since been removed—and to this he clung fast in spite of the jerk of his arrested body, which threatened to tear away his grip.

But his plight was desperate, nevertheless. He was dangling in space, the hard pavement thirty feet below him, with no possible way of pulling himself up to the roof again. And the hook was so small that there was no place for his other hand. The only way he could cling to it at all was to grasp his wrist with the free hand as a partial relief from the strain upon his arm.

"Hold fast!" called Patsy. "I'm coming."

She sprang up the steps, through the boy's room and into the hallway. There she quickly perceived the ladder, and mounted it to the roof. Taking in the situation at a glance she ran with steady steps down the sloping roof to where the plank lay, and stepped out upon it far enough to

AUNT JANE'S NIECES.

see the boy dangling beside her. Then she decided instantly what to do.

"Hang on!" she called, and returning to the
roof dragged the end of the plank to a position
directly over the hook. Then she lay flat upon
it, an arm on either side of the plank, and reach-
ing down seized one of the boy's wrists firmly in
each hand.

"Now, then," said she, "let go the hook."

"If I do," answered the boy, his white face
upturned to hers, "I'll drag you down with me."

"No you won't. I'm very strong, and I'm
sure I can save you. Let go," she said, im-
peratively.

"I'm not afraid to die," replied the boy, his
voice full of bitterness. "Take away your hands,
and I'll drop."

But Patsy gripped him more firmly than ever.

"Don't be a fool!" she cried. "There's no
danger whatever, if you do just what I tell you."

His eyes met hers in a mute appeal; but suddenly he gained confidence, and resolved to trust
her. In any event, he could not cling to the hook
much longer.

He released his hold, and swung in mid-air just beneath the plank, where the girl lay holding him by his wrists.

"Now, then," she said, quietly, "when I lift you up, grab the edges of the plank."

Patrica's strength was equal to her courage, and under the excitement of that desperate moment she did what few other girls of her size could ever have accomplished. She drew the boy up until his eager hands caught the edges of the plank, and gripped it firmly. Then she released him and crept a little back toward the roof.

"Now swing your legs up and you're safe!" she cried.

He tried to obey, but his strength was failing him, and he could do no more than touch the plank with his toes.

"Once more," called the girl.

This time she caught his feet as they swung upward, and drew his legs around the plank.

"Can you climb up, now?" she asked, anxiously.

"I'll try," he panted.

The plank upon which this little tragedy was

being enacted was in full view of the small garden where Aunt Jane loved to sit in her chair and enjoy the flowers and the sunshine. She could not see Kenneth's wing at all, but she could see the elevated plank leading from the roof to the oak tree, and for several days had been puzzled by its appearance and wondered for what purpose it was there.

Today, as she sat talking with John Merrick and Silas Watson, she suddenly gave a cry of surprise, and following her eyes the two men saw Kenneth step out upon the roof, fall, and slide over the edge. For a moment all three remained motionless, seized with fear and consternation, and then they saw Patsy appear and run down to the plank.

This they watched her move, and saw her lie down upon it.

"She's trying to save him—he must be caught somewhere!" cried the lawyer, and both men started at full speed to reach the spot by the round-about paths through the garden.

Aunt Jane sat still and watched. Suddenly the form of the boy swung into view beneath the

AUNT JANE'S NIECES.

plank, dangling from the girl's outstretched
arms. The woman caught her breath, wondering
what would happen next. Patricia drew him up,
until he seized the plank with his hands. Then
the girl crept back a little, and as the boy swung
his feet upward she caught them and twined his
legs over the plank.

And now came the supreme struggle. The
girl could do little more to help him. He must
manage to clamber upon the top of the plank
himself.

Ordinarily Kenneth might have done this
easily; but now his nerves were all unstrung, and
he was half exhausted by the strain of the past
few minutes. Almost he did it; but not quite.
The next effort would be even weaker. But now
Patricia walked out upon the plank and Aunt
Jane saw her lean down, grasp the boy's collar
and drag him into a position of safety.

"Bravely done!" she murmured, but even as
the sound came from her lips the girl upon the
bridge seemed in the exertion of the struggle to
lose her balance. She threw out her arms,

leaned sidewise, and then fell headlong into the chasm and disappeared from view.

Aunt Jane's agonized scream brought Phibbs running to her side. At a glance she saw that her mistress had fainted, and looking hastily around to discover the cause she observed the boy crawl slowly across the plank, reach the tree, and slide down its trunk to pass out of view behind the high hedge.

"Drat the boy!" growled the old servant, angrily, "he'll be the death of Miss Jane, yet."

# CHAPTER XVI.

### GOOD RESULTS.

Uncle John could not run so swiftly as the lawyer, but he broke through a gap in the hedge and arrived at a point just beneath the plank at the same time that Silas Watson did.

One glance showed them the boy safely perched on top of the plank, but the girl was bending backward. She threw out her arms in a vain endeavor to save herself, and with a low cry toppled and plunged swiftly toward the ground.

There was little time for the men to consider their actions. Involuntarily they tried to catch Patricia, whose body struck them sharply, felling them to the ground, and then bounded against the hedge and back to the pavement.

When, half dazed, they scrambled to their

feet, the girl lay motionless before them, a stream
of red blood welling from a deep cut in her for-
head, her eyes closed as if in sleep.

A moment more and the boy was kneeling
beside her, striving to stay the bleeding with his
handkerchief.

"Do something! For God's sake try to do
something," he wailed, piteously. "Can't you
see she's killed herself to save me?"

Uncle John knelt down and took the still
form in his arms.

"Quiet, my lad," he said. "She isn't dead.
Get Nora, and fetch the doctor as soon as you
can."

The boy was gone instantly, his agony relieved by the chance of action, and followed by
the lawyer, Uncle John carried his niece to the
rose chamber and laid her upon her white bed.

Misery met them, then, and following her
came Louise and Beth, full of horror and pity for
the victim of the dreadful accident.

Jane Merrick had promptly recovered consciousness, for fainting spells were foreign to her

nature. Her first words to Phibbs, who was bending over her, were:

"Is she dead?"

"Who, Miss Jane?"

"Patricia."

"I don't know, Miss Jane. Why should she be dead?"

"Run, you idiot! Run at once and find out. Ask my brother—ask anyone—if Patricia is dead!"

And so Phibbs came to the rose chamber and found the little group bending over the girl's unconscious form.

"Is she dead, sir? Miss Jane wants to know," said the old servant, in awe-struck tones.

"No," answered Uncle John, gravely. "She isn't dead, I'm sure; but I can't tell how badly she is hurt. One of her legs—the right one—is broken, I know, for I felt it as I carried the child in my arms; but we must wait until the doctor comes before I can tell more."

Misery was something of a nurse, it seemed, and with the assistance of Louise, who proved most helpful in the emergency, she bathed the wound in the girl's forehead and bandaged it as well as she was able. Between them the women also removed Patricia's clothing and got her into bed, where she lay white and still unconscious, but breathing so softly that they knew she was yet alive.

The doctor was not long in arriving, for Kenneth forced him to leap upon Nora's back and race away to Elmhurst, while the boy followed as swiftly as he could on the doctor's sober cob.

Dr. Eliel was only a country practitioner, but his varied experiences through many years had given him a practical knowledge of surgery, and after a careful examination of Patricia's injuries he was able to declare that she would make a fine recovery.

"Her leg is fractured, and she's badly bruised," he reported to Aunt Jane, who sent for him as soon as he could leave the sick room. "But I do not think she has suffered any internal injuries, and the wound on her forehead is a mere nothing. So, with good care, I expect the young lady to get along nicely."

"Do everything you can for her," said the woman, earnestly. "You shall be well paid, Dr. Eliel."

Before Patricia recovered her senses the doctor had sewn up her forehead and set the fractured limb, so that she suffered little pain from the first.

Louise and Beth hovered over her constantly, ministering to every possible want and filled with tenderest sympathy for their injured cousin. The accident seemed to draw them out of their selfishness and petty intrigues and discovered in them the true womanly qualities that had lurked beneath the surface.

Patsy was not allowed to talk, but she smiled gratefully at her cousins, and the three girls seemed suddenly drawn nearer together than any of them would have thought possible a few hours before.

The boy paced constantly up and down outside Patricia's door, begging everyone who left the room, for news of the girl's condition. All his reserve and fear of women seemed to have melted away as if by magic. Even Beth and

Louise were questioned eagerly, and they, having learned the story of Patricia's brave rescue of the boy, were very gentle with him and took pains not to frighten or offend him.

Toward evening Louise asked Patricia if she would see Kenneth for a moment, and the girl nodded a ready assent.

He came in awkward and trembling, glancing fearfully at the bandaged forehead and the still white face. But Patricia managed to smile reassuringly, and held out a little hand for him to take. The boy grasped it in both his own, and held it for several minutes while he stood motionless beside her, his wide eyes fixed intently upon her own.

Then Louise sent him away, and he went to his room and wept profusely, and then quieted down into a sort of dull stupor.

The next morning Uncle John dragged him away from Patricia's door and forced him to play chess. The boy lost every game, being inattentive and absorbed in thought, until finally Uncle John gave up the attempt to amuse him and settled himself on the top stair for a quiet smoke. The boy turned to the table, and took a sheet of paper from the drawer . For an hour, perhaps, neither of these curious friends spoke a word, but at the end of that time Uncle John arose and knocked the ashes from his pipe. Kenneth did not notice him. The man approached the table and looked over the boy's shoulder, uttering an exclamation of surprise. Upon the paper appeared a cleverly drawn pencil sketch of Patricia lying in her bed, a faint smile upon her face and her big blue eyes turned pleasantly upon a shadowy form that stood beside her holding her hand. The likeness was admirable, and if there were faults in the perspective and composition Uncle John did not recognize them.

He gave a low whistle and turned thoughtfully away, and the young artist was so absorbed that he did not even look up.

Strolling away to the stables, Uncle John met old Donald, who enquired:

"How is Miss Patsy this morning, sir?" It was the name she had given, and preferred to be called by.

"She's doing finely," said Uncle John.

"A brave girl, sir !"

"Yes, Donald."

"And the boy ?"

"Why, he seems changed, in some way, Donald. Not so nervous and wild as usual, you know. I've just left him drawing a picture. Curious. A good picture, too."

"Ah, he can do that, sir, as well as a real artist."

"Have you known him to draw, before this?"

"Why, he's always at it, sir, in his quieter moods. I've got a rare good likeness o' myself, as he did long ago, in the harness room."

"May I see it?"

"With pleasure, sir."

Donald led the way to the harness-room, and took from the cupboard the precious board he had so carefully preserved.

Uncle John glanced at it and laughed aloud. He could well appreciate the humor of the sketch, which Donald never had understood, and the caricature was as clever as it was amusing. He handed the treasure back to Donald and went away even more thoughtful than before.

A few days later a large package arrived at Elmhurst addressed to Kenneth Forbes, and Oscar carried it at once to the boy's room, who sat for an hour looking at it in silent amazement. Then he carefully unwrapped it, and found it to contain a portable easel, a quantity of canvas and drawing-paper, paints and oils of every description (mostly all unknown to him) and pencils, brushes and water colors in profusion.

Kenneth's heart bounded with joy. Here was wealth, indeed, greater than he had ever hoped for. He puzzled his brain for weeks to discover how this fairy gift had ever come to him, but he was happier in its possession than he had ever been before in all his life.

Patricia improved rapidly. Had it not been for the broken leg she would have been out of the house in a week, as good as ever; but broken limbs take time to heal, and Dr. Eliel would not permit the girl to leave her bed until ten days had passed.

Meantime everyone delighted to attend her. Louise and Beth sat with her for hours, reading or working, for the rose chamber was cheery and pleasant, and its big windows opened upon the prettiest part of the gardens. The two girls were even yet suspicious of one another, each striving to win an advantage with Aunt Jane; but neither had the slightest fear that Patricia would ever interfere with their plans. So they allowed their natural inclinations to pet and admire the heroine of the hour full sway, and Patsy responded so sweetly and frankly to their advances that they came to love her dearly, and wondered why they had not discovered from the first how lovable their Irish cousin could be.

Kenneth, also came daily to the sick room for a visit, and Patsy had a way of drawing the boy out and making him talk that was really irresistible. After his fairy gift arrived he could not help telling the girls all about it, and then he brought the things down and displayed them, and promised Patsy he would make a picture of the garden for her.

Then, after the girl got better, he brought his easel down to her room, where she could watch him work, and began upon the picture, while

the cousins joined him in speculations as to who
the mysterious donor could be.

"At first," said Kenneth, "I thought it was
Mr. Watson, for he's alway been very good to
me; but he says he knows nothing about it. Then
I though it might be Uncle John; but Uncle John
is too poor to afford such an expensive present."

"I don't believe he has a penny in the world,"
said Louise, who sat by with some needle-work.

"All he owns," remarked Beth, with a laugh,
"is an extra necktie, slightly damaged."

"But he's a dear old man," said Patsy, loy-
ally, "and I'm sure he would have given all those
things to Kenneth had he been able."

"Then who was it?" asked the boy.

"Why, Aunt Jane, to be sure," declared
Patsy.

The boy scowled, and shook his head.

"She wouldn't do anything to please me, even
to save her life," he growled. "She hates me,
I know that well enough."

"Oh, no; I'm sure she doesn't," said Patsy.
"Aunt Jane has a heap of good in her; but you've
got to dig for it, like you do for gold. 'Twould

be just like her to make you this present and keep it a secret."

"If she really did it," replied the boy, slowly, "and it seems as if she is the only one I know who could afford such a gift, it stands to reason that either Uncle John or Mr. Watson asked her to, and she did it to please them. I've lived here for years, and she has never spoken a kindly word to me or done me a kindly act. It isn't likely she'd begin now, is it?"

Unable to make a reassuring reply, Patsy remained silent, and the boy went on with his work. He first outlined the picture in pencil, and then filled it in with water color. They all expressed admiration for the drawing, but the color effect was so horrible that even Patsy found no words to praise it, and the boy in a fit of sudden anger tore the thing to shreds and so destroyed it.

"But I must have my picture, anyhow," said the girl. "Make it in pen and ink or pencil, Ken. and I'm sure it will be beautiful."

"You need instruction, to do water color properly," suggested Louise.

"Then I can never do it," he replied, bitterly.

AUNT JANE'S NIECES.

But he adopted Patsy's suggestion and sketched the garden very prettily in pen and ink. By the time the second picture was completed Patsy had received permission to leave her room, which she did in Aunt Jane's second-best wheel chair.

Her first trip was to Aunt Jane's own private garden, where the invalid, who had not seen her niece since the accident, had asked her to come.

Patsy wanted Kenneth to wheel her, but the boy, with a touch of his old surly demeanor, promptly refused to meet Jane Merrick face to face. So Beth wheeled the chair and Louise walked by Patsy's side, and soon the three nieces reached their aunt's retreat.

Aunt Jane was not in an especially amiable mood.

"Well, girl, how do you like being a fool?" she demanded, as Patsy's chair came to a stand just opposite her own.

"It feels so natural that I don't mind it," replied Patsy, laughing.

"You might have killed yourself, and all for nothing," continued the old woman, querulously.

AUNT JANE'S NIECES.

Patsy looked at her pityingly. Her aunt's face had aged greatly in the two weeks, and the thin gray hair seemed now almost white.

"Are you feeling better, dear?" asked the girl.

"I shall never be better," said Jane Merrick, sternly. "The end is not far off now."

"Oh, I'm sorry to hear you say that!" said Patsy; "but I hope it is not true. Why, here are we four newly found relations all begining to get acquainted, and to love one another, and we can't have our little party broken up, auntie dear."

"Five of us—five relations," cried Uncle John, coming around the corner of the hedge. "Don't I count, Patsy, you rogue? Why you're looking as bright and as bonny as can be. I wouldn't be surprised if you could toddle."

"Not yet," she answered, cheerfully. "But I'm doing finely, Uncle John, and it won't be long before I can get about as well as ever."

"And to think," said Aunt Jane, bitterly, "that all this trouble was caused by that miser-

186

able boy! If I knew where to send him he'd not stay at Elmhurst a day longer."

"Why, he's my best friend, aunt," announced Patsy, quietly. "I don't think I could be happy at Elmhurst without Kenneth."

"He has quite reformed," said Louise, "and seems like a very nice boy."

"He's a little queer, yet, at times," added Beth, "but not a bit rude, as he used to be."

Aunt Jane looked from one to the other in amazement. No one had spoken so kindly of the boy before in years. And Uncle John, with a thoughtful look on his face, said slowly:

"The fact is, Jane, you've never given the boy a chance. On the contrary, you nearly ruined him by making a hermit of him and giving him no schooling to speak of and no society except that of servants. He was as wild as a hawk when I first came, but these girls are just the sort of companions he needs, to soften him and make him a man. I've no doubt he'll come out all right, in the end."

"Perhaps you'd like to adopt him yourself,

John," sneered the woman, furious at this praise of the one person she so greatly disliked.

Her brother drew his hands from his pockets, looked around in a helpless and embarrassed way, and then tried fumblingly to fill his pipe.

"I ain't in the adopting business, Jane," he answered meekly. "And if I was," with a quaint smile, "I'd adopt one or two of these nieces o' mine, instead of Tom Bradley's nephew. If Bradley hadn't seen you, Jane, and loved your pretty face when you were young, Kenneth Forbes would now be the owner of Elmhurst. Did you ever think of that?"

Did she ever think of it? Why, it was this very fact that made the boy odious to her. The woman grew white with rage.

"John Merrick, leave my presence."

"All right, Jane."

He stopped to light his pipe, and then slowly walked away, leaving an embarrassed group behind him.

Patsy, however, was equal to the occasion. She began at once to chatter about Dr. Eliel, and the scar that would always show on her forehead;

and how surprised the Major, her father, would be when he returned from the visit to his colonel and found his daughter had been through the wars herself, and bore the evidence of honorable wounds. Louise gracefully assisted her cousin to draw Aunt Jane into a more genial mood, and between them they presently succeeded. The interview that had begun so unfortunately ended quite pleasantly, and when Patricia returned to her room her aunt bade her adieu almost tenderly.

"In fact," said Louise to Beth, in the privacy of the latter's chamber, "I'm getting rather worried over Aunt Jane's evident weakness for our Cousin Patsy. Once or twice today I caught a look in her eye when she looked at Patsy that she has never given either you or me. The Irish girl may get the money yet."

"Nonsense," said Beth. "She has said she wouldn't accept a penny of it, and I'm positive she'll keep her word."

# CHAPTER XVII.

### AUNT JANE'S HEIRESS.

"Silas," said Aunt Jane to her lawyer, the next morning after her interview with Patsy, "I'm ready to have you draw up my will."

Mr. Watson gave a start of astonishment. In his own mind he had arrived at the conclusion that the will would never be executed, and to have Miss Merrick thus suddenly declare her decision was enough to startle even the lawyer's natural reserve.

"Very well, Jane," he said, briefly.

They were alone in the invalid's morning room, Phibbs having been asked to retire.

"There is no use disguising the fact, Silas, that I grow weaker every day, and the numbness is creeping nearer and nearer to my heart," said Miss Merrick, in her usual even tones. "It is folly for me to trifle with these few days of grace yet allowed me, and I have fully made up my mind as to the disposition of my property."

"Yes?" he said, enquiringly, and drew from his pocket a pencil and paper.

"I shall leave to my niece Louise five thous‧and dollars."

"Yes, Jane," jotting down the memorandum.

"And to Elizabeth a like sum."

The lawyer seemed disappointed. He tapped the pencil against his teeth, musingly, for a moment, and then wrote down the amount.

"Also to my brother, John Merrick, the sum of five thousand dollars," she resumed.

"To your brother?"

"Yes. That should be enough to take care of him as long as he lives. He seems quite simpie in his tastes, and he is an old man."

The lawyer wrote it down.

"All my other remaining property, both real and personal, I shall leave to my niece, Patricia Doyle."

"Jane!"

"Did you hear me?"

# AUNT JANE'S NIECES.

"Yes."

"Then do as I bid you, Silas Watson."

He leaned back in his chair and looked at her thoughtfully.

"I am not only your lawyer, Jane; I am also your friend and counsellor. Do you realize what this bequest means?" he asked, gently.

"It means that Patricia will inherit Elmhurst —and a fortune besides. Why not, Silas? I liked the child from the first. She's frank and open and brave, and will do credit to my judgment."

"She is very young and unsophisticated," said the lawyer, "and of all your nieces she will least appreciate your generosity."

"You are to be my executor, and manage the estate until the girl comes of age. You will see that she is properly educated and fitted for her station in life. As for appreciation, or gratitude, I don't care a snap of my finger for such fol-de-rol."

The lawyer sighed.

"But the boy, Jane? You seem to have forgotten him," he said.

"Drat the boy! I've done enough for him already."

"Wouldn't Tom like you to provide for Kenneth in some way, however humbly?"

She glared at him angrily.

"How do you know what Tom would like, after all these years?" she asked, sternly. "And how should I know, either? The money is mine, and the boy is nothing to me. Let him shift for himself."

"There is a great deal of money, Jane," declared the lawyer, impressively. "We have been fortunate in our investments, and you have used but little of your ample income. To spare fifty thousand dollars to Kenneth, who is Tom's sole remaining relative, would be no hardship to Patricia. Indeed, she would scarcely miss it."

"You remind me of something, Silas," she said, looking at him with friendly eyes. "Make a memorandum of twenty thousand dollars to Silas Watson. You have been very faithful to my interests and have helped materially to increase my fortune."

"Thank you, Jane."

He wrote down the amount as calmly as he
had done the others.

"And the boy?" he asked, persistently.

Aunt Jane sighed wearily, and leaned against
her pillows.

"Give the boy two thousand," she said.

"Make it ten, Jane."

"I'll make it five, and not a penny more," she
rejoined. "Now leave me, and prepare the paper
at once. I want to sign it today, if possible."

He bowed gravely, and left the room.

Toward evening the lawyer came again, bringing with him a notary from the village. Dr. Eliel,
who had come to visit Patricia, was also called
into Jane Merrick's room, and after she had carefully read the paper in their presence the mistress
of Elmhurst affixed her signature to the document which transferred the great estate to the
little Irish girl, and the notary and the doctor
solemnly witnessed it and retired.

"Now, Silas," said the old woman, with a
sigh of intense relief, "I can die in peace."

Singularly enough, the signing of the will
seemed not to be the end for Jane Merrick, but

AUNT JANE'S NIECES.

the beginning of an era of unusual comfort. On
the following morning she awakened brighter
than usual, having passed a good night, freed
from the worries and anxieties that had beset
her for weeks. She felt more like her old self
than at any time since the paralysis had overtaken her, and passed the morning most enjoy-
ably in her sunshiney garden. Here Patricia
was also brought in her wheel chair by Beth, who
then left the two invalids together.

They conversed genially enough, for a time,
until an unfortunate remark of Aunt Jane's which
seemed to asperse her father's character aroused
Patricia's ire. Then she loosened her tongue, and
in her voluable Irish way berated her aunt until
poor Phibbs stood aghast at such temerity, and
even Mr. Watson, who arrived to enquire after
his client and friend, was filled with amazement.

He cast a significant look at Miss Merrick,
who answered it in her usual emphatic way.

"Patricia is quite right, Silas," she declared,
"and I deserve all that she has said. If the girl
were fond enough of me to defend me as heartily

195

as she does her father, I would be very proud, indeed."

Patricia cooled at once, and regarded her aunt with a sunny smile.

"Forgive me!" she begged. "I know you did not mean it, and I was wrong to talk to you in such a way."

So harmony was restored, and Mr. Watson wondered more and more at this strange perversion of the old woman's character. Heretofore any opposition had aroused in her intense rage and a fierce antagonism, but now she seemed delighted to have Patsy fly at her, and excused the girl's temper instead of resenting it.

But Patsy was a little ashamed of herself this morning, realizing perhaps that Aunt Jane had been trying to vex her, just to enjoy her indignant speeches; and she also realized the fact that her aunt was old and suffering, and not wholly responsible for her aggravating and somewhat malicious observations. So she firmly resolved not to be so readily entrapped again, and was so bright and cheery during the next hour that Aunt Jane smiled more than once, and at one time actually laughed at her niece's witty repartee.

After that it became the daily program for Patsy to spend her mornings in Aunt Jane's little garden, and although they sometimes clashed, and, as Phibbs told Beth, "had dreadful fights," they both enjoyed these hours very much.

The two girls became rather uneasy during the days their cousin spent in the society of Aunt Jane. Even the dreadful accounts they received from Phibbs failed wholly to reassure them, and Louise redoubled her solicitious attentions to her aunt in order to offset the influence Patricia seemed to be gaining over her.

Louise had also become, by this time, the managing housekeeper of the establishment, and it was certain that Aunt Jane looked upon her eldest and most competent niece with much favor.

Beth, with all her friends to sing her praises, seemed to make less headway with her aunt than either of the others, and gradually she sank into a state of real despondency.

"I've done the best I could," she wrote her mother, "but I'm not as clever as Louise nor as

197

amusing as Patricia; so Aunt Jane pays little attention to me. She's a dreadful old woman, and I can't bring myself to appear to like her. That probably accounts for my failure; but I may as well stay on here until something happens."

In a fortnight more Patricia abandoned her chair and took to crutches, on which she hobbled everywhere as actively as the others walked. She affected her cousins' society more, from this time, and Aunt Jane's society less, for she had come to be fond of the two girls who had nursed her so tenderly, and it was natural that a young girl would prefer to be with those of her own age rather than a crabbed old woman like Aunt Jane.

Kenneth also now became Patsy's faithful companion, for the boy had lost his former bashfulness and fear of girls, and had grown to feel at ease even in the society of Beth and Louise. The four had many excursions and picnics into the country together; but Kenneth and Patsy were recognized as especial chums, and the other girls did not interfere in their friendship except to tease them, occasionally, in a good natured way.

## AUNT JANE'S NIECES.

The boy's old acquaintances could hardly recognize him as the same person they had known before Patricia's adventure on the plank. His fits of gloomy abstraction and violent bursts of temper had alike vanished, or only prevailed at brief intervals. Nor was he longer rude and unmannerly to those with whom he came in contact. Awkward he still was, and lacking in many graces that education and good society can alone confer; but he was trying hard to be, as he confided to old Uncle John, "like other people," and succeeded in adapting himself very well to his new circumstances.

Although he had no teacher, as yet, he had begun to understand color a little, and succeeded in finishing one or two water-color sketches which Patsy, who knew nothing at all of such things, pronounced "wonderfully fine." Of course the boy blushed with pleasure and was encouraged to still greater effort.

The girl was also responsible for Kenneth's sudden advancement in the household at Elmhurst.

One day she said calmly to Aunt Jane:

"I've invited Kenneth to dinner this evening."

The woman flew angry in an instant.

"Who gave you such authority?" she demanded.

"No one. I just took it," said Patsy, saucily.

"He shall not come," declared Aunt Jane, sternly. "I'll have no interference from you, Miss, with my household arrangements. Phibbs, call Louise!"

Patsy's brow grew dark. Presently Louise appeared.

"Instruct the servants to forbid that boy to enter my dining room this evening," she said to Louise.

"Also, Louise," said Patsy, "tell them not to lay a plate for me, and ask Oscar to be ready with the wagon at five o'clock. I'm going home."

Louise hesitated, and looked from Miss Jane to Patsy, and back again. They were glaring upon each other like two gorgons.

Then she burst into laughter; she could not help it, the sight was too ridiculous. A moment later Patsy was laughing, too, and then Aunt Jane allowed a grim smile to cross her features.

"Never mind, Louise," she said, with remarkable cheerfulness; "We'll compromise matters."

"How?" asked Patsy.

"By putting a plate for Kenneth," said her aunt, cooly. "I imagine I can stand his society for one evening."

So the matter was arranged to Patricia's satisfaction, and the boy came to dinner, trembling and unhappy at first, but soon placed at ease by the encouragements of the three girls. Indeed, he behaved so well, in the main, and was so gentle and unobstrusive, that Aunt Jane looked at him with surprise, and favored him with one or two speeches which he answered modestly and well.

Patsy was radiant with delight, and the next day Aunt Jane remarked casually that she did not object to the boy's presence at dinner, at all, and he could come whenever he liked.

This arrangement gave great pleasure to both Uncle John and Mr. Watson, the latter of whom

was often present at the "state dinner," and both
men congratulated Patsy upon the distinct vic-
tory she had won. No more was said about her
leaving Elmhurst. The Major wrote that he
was having a splendid time with the colonel, and
begged for an extension of his vacation, to which
Patsy readily agreed, she being still unable on account of her limb to return to her work at Madam
Borne's.

And so the days glided pleasantly by, and August came to find a happy company of young folks
at old Elmhurst, with Aunt Jane wonderfully
improved in health and Uncle John beaming complacently upon everyone he chanced to meet.

# CHAPTER XVIII.

It was Lawyer Watson's suggestion that she was being unjust to Beth and Louise, in encouraging them to hope they might inherit Elmhurst, that finally decided Aunt Jane to end all misunderstandings and inform her nieces of the fact that she had made a final disposition of her property.

So one morning she sent word asking them all into her room, and when the nieces appeared they found Uncle John and the lawyer already in their aunt's presence. There was an air of impressive formality pervading the room, although Miss Merrick's brother, at least, was as ignorant as her nieces of the reason why they had been summoned.

Patsy came in last, hobbling actively on her

crutches, although the leg was now nearly recovered, and seated herself somewhat in the rear
of the apartment.

Aunt Jane looked into one expectant face after another with curious interest, and then broke
the silence by saying, gravely, but in more gentle tones than she was accustomed to use:

"I believe, young ladies, that you have understood from the first my strongest reason for inviting you to visit Elmhurst this summer. I am
old, and must soon pass away, and instead of
leaving you and your parents, who would be my
legitimate heirs, to squabble over my property
when I am gone, I decided to excute a will bequeathing my estate to some one who would take
proper care of it and maintain it in a creditable
manner. I had no personal acquaintance with
any of you, but judged that one out of the three
might serve my purpose, and therefore invited
you all here."

By this time the hearts of Louise and Beth
were fluttering with excitement, and even Patsy
looked interested. Uncle John sat a little apart,
watching them with an amused smile upon his

face, and the lawyer sat silent with his eyes fixed upon a pattern in the rug.

"In arriving at a decision, which I may say I have succeeded in doing," continued Aunt Jane, calmly, "I do not claim to have acted with either wisdom or discernment. I have simply followed my own whim, as I have the right to do, and selected the niece I prefer to become my heiress. You cannot accuse of injustice, because none of you had a right to expect anything of me; but I will say this, that I am well pleased with all three of you, and now wish that I had taken pains to form your acquaintance earlier in life. You might have cheered my old age, and rendered it less lonely and dull."

"Well said, Jane," remarked Uncle John, nodding his head approvingly.

She did not notice the interruption, but presently continued:

"Some days ago I asked my lawyer, Mr. Watson, to draw up my will. It was at once prepared and signed, and now stands as my last will and testament. I have given to you, Louise, the sum of five thousand dollars."

AUNT JANE'S NIECES.

Louise laughed nervously, and threw out her hands with an indifferent gesture.

"Many thanks, Aunt," she said, lightly.

"To you, Beth," continued Miss Merrick, "I have given the same sum."

Beth's heart sank, and tears forced themselves into her eyes in spite of her efforts to restrain them. She said nothing.

Aunt Jane turned to her brother.

"I have also provided for you, John, in the sum of five thousand dollars."

"Me!" he exclaimed, astounded. "Why, suguration, Jane, I don't—"

"Silence!" she cried, sternly. "I expect neither thanks nor protests. If you take care of the money, John, it will last you as long as you live."

Uncle John laughed. He doubled up in his chair and rocked back and forth, shaking his little round body as if he had met with the most amusing thing that had ever happened in his life. Aunt Jane stared at him, while Louise and Beth looked their ashonishment, but Patsy's clear

206

laughter rang above Uncle John's gasping chuckles.

"I hope, dear Uncle," said she, mischievously, "that when poor Aunt Jane is gone you'll be able to buy a new necktie."

He looked at her whimsically, and wiped the tears from his eyes.

"Thank you, Jane," said the little man to his sister. "It's a lot of money, and I'll be proud to own it."

"Why did you laugh?" demanded Aunt Jane.

"I just happened to think that our old Dad once said I'd never be worth a dollar in all my life. What would he say now, Jane, if he knew I stood good to have five thousand—if I can manage to outlive you?"

She turned from him with an expression of scorn.

"In addition to these bequests," said she, "I have left five thousand to the boy and twenty thousand to Mr. Watson. The remainder of the property will go to Patricia."

For a moment the room was intensely still. Then Patricia said, with quiet determination:

"You may as well make another will, Aunt. I'll not touch a penny of your money."

"Why not?" asked the woman, almost fiercely.

"You have been kind to me, and you mean well," said Patricia. "I would rather not tell you my reasons."

"I demand to know them!"

"Ah, aunt; can't you understand, without my speaking?"

"No," said the other; but a flush crossed her pale cheek, nevertheless.

Patsy arose and stumped to a position directly in front of Jane Merrick, where she rested on her crutches. Her eyes were bright and full of indignation, and her plain little face was so white that every freckle showed distinctly.

"There was a time, years ago," she began in a low voice, "when you were very rich and your sister Violet, my mother, was very poor. Her health was bad, and she had me to care for, while my father was very ill with a fever. She was proud, too, and for herself she would never have begged a penny of anyone; but for my sake she asked her rich sister to loan her a little money to tide her over her period of want. What did you do, Jane Merrick, you who lived in a beautiful mansion, and had more money than you could use? You insulted her, telling her she belonged to a family of beggars, and that none of them could wheedle your money away from you!"

"It was true," retorted the elder woman, stubbornly. "They were after me like a drove of wolves—every Merrick of them all—and they would have ruined me if I had let them bleed me as they wished."

"So far as my mother is concerned, that's a lie," said Patsy, quietly. "She never appealed to you but that once, but worked as bravely as she could to earn money in her own poor way. The result was that she died, and I was left to the care of strangers until my father was well enough to support me."

She paused, and again the room seemed unnaturally still.

"I'm sorry, girl," said Aunt Jane, at last, in trembling tones. "I was wrong. I see it now, and I am sorry I refused Violet."

# AUNT JANE'S NIECES.

"Then I forgive you!" said Patsy, impulsively. "I forgive you all, Aunt Jane; for through your own selfishness you cut yourself off from all your family—from all who might have loved you—and you have lived all these years a solitary and loveless life. There'll be no grudge of mine to follow you to the grave, Aunt Jane. "But," her voice hardening, "I'll never touch a penny of the money that was denied my poor dead mother. Thank God the old Dad and I are independent, and can earn our own living."

Uncle John came to where Patsy stood and put both arms around her, pressing her—crutches and all—close to his breast. Then he released her, and without a word stalked from the room.

"Leave me, now," said Aunt Jane, in a husky voice. "I want time to think."

Patricia hobbled forward, placed one hand caressingly upon the gray head, and then bent and kissed Aunt Jane's withered cheek.

"That's right," she whispered. "Think it over, dear. It's all past and done, now, and I'm sorry I had to hurt you. But—not a penny, aunt —remember, not a penny will I take!"

Then she left the room, followed by Louise and Beth, both of whom were glad to be alone that they might conquer their bitter disappointment.

Louise, however, managed to accept the matter philosophically, as the following extract from her letter to her mother will prove:

"After all, it isn't so bad as it might be, mater, dear," she wrote. "I'll get five thousand, at the very worst, and that will help us on our way considerably. But I am quite sure that Patsy means just what she says, and that she will yet induce Aunt Jane to alter her will. In that case I believe the estate will either be divided between Beth and me, or I will get it all. Anyway, I shall stay here and play my best cards until the game is finished."

# CHAPTER XIX.

## DUPLICITY.

Aunt Jane had a bad night, as might have been expected after her trials of the previous day.

She sent for Patricia early in the forenoon, and when the girl arrived she was almost shocked by the change in her aunt's appearance. The invalid's face seemed drawn and gray, and she lay upon her cushions breathing heavily and without any appearance of vitality or strength. Even the sharpness and piercing quality of her hard gray eyes was lacking and the glance she cast at her niece was rather pleading than defiant.

"I want you to reconsider your decision of yesterday, Patricia," she begun.

"Don't ask me to do that, aunt," replied the girl, firmly. "My mind is fully made up."

AUNT JANE'S NIECES.

"I have made mistakes, I know," continued the woman feebly; "but I want to do the right thing, at last."

"Then I will show you how," said Patricia, quickly. "You mustn't think me impertinent, aunt, for I don't mean to be so at all. But tell me; why did you wish to leave me your money?"

"Because your nature is quite like my own, child, and I admire your independence and spirit."

"But my cousins are much more deserving," said she, thoughtfully. "Louise is very sweet and amiable, and loves you more than I do, while Beth is the most sensible and practical girl I have ever known."

"It may be so," returned Aunt Jane, impatiently; "but I have left each a legacy, Patricia, and you alone are my choice for the mistress of Elmhurst. I told you yesterday I should not try to be just. I mean to leave my property according to my personal desire, and no one shall hinder me." This last with a spark of her old vigor.

"But that is quite wrong, aunt, and if you desire me to inherit your wealth you will be disappointed. A moment ago you said you wished to do the right thing, at last. Don't you know what that is?"

"Perhaps you will tell me," said Aunt Jane, curiously.

"With pleasure," returned Patsy. "Mr. Bradley left you this property because he loved you, and love blinded him to all sense of justice. Such an estate should not have passed into the hands of aliens because of a lover's whim. He should have considered his own flesh and blood."

"There was no one but his sister, who at that time was not married and had no son," explained Aunt Jane, calmly. "But he did not forget her and asked me to look after Katherine Bradley in case she or her heirs ever needed help. I have done so. When his mother died, I had the boy brought here, and he has lived here ever since."

"But the property ought to be his," said Patricia, earnestly. "It would please me beyond measure to have you make your will in his favor, and you would be doing the right thing at last."

"I won't," said Aunt Jane, angrily.

"It would also be considerate and just to the

memory of Mr. Bradley," continued the girl. "What's going to became of Kenneth?"

"I have left him five thousand," said the woman.

"Not enough to educate him properly," replied Patsy, with a shake of her head. "Why, the boy might become a famous artist, if he had good masters; and a person with an artistic temperament, such as his, should have enough money to be independent of his art."

Aunt Jane coughed, unsympathetically.

"The boy is nothing to me," she said.

"But he ought to have Elmhurst, at least," pleaded the girl. "Won't you leave it to him, Aunt Jane?"

"No."

"Then do as you please," cried Patsy, flying angry in her turn. "As a matter of justice, the place should never have been yours, and I won't accept a dollar of the money if I starve to death!"

"Think of your father," suggested Aunt Jane, cunningly.

"Ah, I've done that," said the girl, "and I know how many comforts I could buy for the

215

dear Major. Also I'd like to go to a girl's college, like Smith or Wellesley, and get a proper education. But not with your money, Aunt Jane. It would burn my fingers. Always I would think that if you had not been hard and miserly this same money would have saved my mother's life. No! I loathe your money. Keep it or throw it to the dogs, if you won't give it to the boy it belongs to. But don't you dare to will your selfish hoard to me."

"Let us change the subject, Patricia."

"Will you change your will?"

"No."

"Then I won't talk to you. I'm angry and hurt, and if I stay here I'll say things I shall be sorry for."

With these words she marched out of the room, her cheeks flaming, and Aunt Jane looked after her with admiring eyes.

"She's right," she whispered to herself. "It's just as I'd do under the same circumstances!"

This interview was but the beginning of a series that lasted during the next fortnight, during which time the invalid persisted in sending for Patricia and fighting the same fight over and over again. Always the girl pleaded for Kenneth to inherit, and declared she would not accept the money and Elmhurst; and always Aunt Jane stubbornly refused to consider the boy and tried to tempt the girl with pictures of the luxury and pleasure that riches would bring her.

The interviews were generally short and spirited, however, and during the intervals Patsy associated more than ever with her cousins, both of whom grew really fond of her.

They fully believed Patricia when she declared she would never accept the inheritance, and although neither Beth nor Louise could understand such foolish sentimentality they were equally overjoyed at the girl's stand and the firmness with which she maintained it. With Patsy out of the field it was quite possible the estate would be divided between her cousins, or even go entire to one or the other of them; and this hope constantly buoyed their spirits and filled their days with interest as they watched the fight between their aunt and their cousin.

AUNT JANE'S NIECES.

Patricia never told them she was pleading so hard for the boy. It would only pain her cousins and make them think she was disloyal to their interests; but she lost no opportunity when with her Aunt Jane of praising Kenneth and proving his ability, and finally she seemed to win her point.

Aunt Jane was really worn out with the constant squabbling with her favorite niece. She had taken a turn for the worse, too, and began to decline rapidly. So, her natural cunning and determination to have her own way enhanced by her illness, the woman decided to deceive Patricia and enjoy her few remaining days in peace.

"Suppose," she said to Mr. Watson, "my present will stands, and after my death the estate becomes the property of Patricia. Can she refuse it?"

"Not legally," returned the lawyer. "It would remain in her name, but under my control, during her minority. When she became of age, however, she could transfer it as she might choose."

"By that time she will have gained more

sense," declared Aunt Jane, much pleased with this aspect of the case, "and it isn't reasonable that having enjoyed a fortune for a time any girl would throw it away. I'll stick to my point, Silas, but I'll try to make Patricia believe she has won me over."

Therefore, the very next time that the girl pleaded with her to make Kenneth her heir, she said, with a clever assumption of resignation:

"Very well, Patricia; you shall have your way. My only desire, child, is to please you, as you well know, and if you long to see Kenneth the owner of Elmhurst I will have a new will drawn in his favor."

Patricia could scarcely believe her ears.

"Do you really mean it, aunt?" she asked, flushing red with pleasure.

"I mean exactly what I say, and now let us cease all bickerings, my dear, and my few remaining days will be peaceful and happy."

Patricia thanked her aunt with eager words, and said, as indeed she felt, that she could almost love Aunt Jane for her final, if dilatory, act of justice.

Mr. Watson chanced to enter the room at that moment, and the girl cried out:

"Tell him, aunt! Let him get the paper ready at once."

"There is no reason for haste," said Aunt Jane, meeting the lawyer's questioning gaze with some embarrassment.

Silas Watson was an honorable and upright man, and his client's frequent doubtful methods had in past years met his severe censure. Yet he had once promised his dead friend, Tom Bradley, that he would serve Jane Merrick faithfully. He had striven to do so, bearing with her faults of character when he found that he could not cor‧ rect them. His influence over her had never been very strong, however, and he had learned that it was the most easy as well as satisfactory method to bow to her iron will.

Her recent questionings had prepared him for some act of duplicity, but he had by no means understood her present object, nor did she mean that he should. So she answered his questioning look by saying:

"I have promised Patricia that you shall draw

a new will, leaving all my estate to Kenneth Forbes, except for the bequests that are mentioned in the present paper."

The lawyer regarded her with amazement. Then his brow darkened, for he thought she was playing with the girl, and was not sincere.

"Tell him to draw up the paper right away, aunt!" begged Patricia, with sparkling eyes.

"As soon as you can, Silas," said the invalid.

"And, aunt, can't you spare a little more to Louise and Beth? It would make them so happy."

"Double the amount I had allowed to each of them," the woman commanded her lawyer.

"Can it all be ready to sign tonight?" asked Patsy, excitedly.

"I'll try, my dear," replied the old lawyer, gravely. Then he turned to Jane Merrick.

"Are you in earnest?" he asked.

Patsy's heart suddenly sank.

"Yes," was the reply. "I am tired of opposing this child's wishes. What do I care what becomes of my money, when I am gone? All that I desire is to have my remaining days peaceful."

The girl spring forward and kissed her rapturously.

"They shall be, aunt!" she cried. "I promise it."

# CHAPTER XX.

## IN THE GARDEN.

From this hour Patsy devoted herself untiringly to Aunt Jane, and filled her days with as much sunshine as her merry ways and happy nature could confer. Yet there was one thing that rendered her uneasy : the paper that Lawyer Watson had so promptly drawn had never yet been signed and witnessed. Her aunt had allowed her to read it, saying she wished the girl to know she had acted in good faith, and Patsy had no fault at all to find with the document. But Aunt Jane was tired, and deferred signing it that evening. The next day no witnesses could be secured, and so another postponement followed, and upon one pretext or another the matter was put off until Patricia became suspicious.

Noting this, Aunt Jane decided to complete

her act of deception. She signed the will in the girl's presence, with Oscar and Susan to witness her signature. Lawyer Watson was not present on this occasion, and as soon as Patsy had left her Miss Merrick tore off the signatures and burned them, wrote "void" in bold letters across the face of the paper, and then, it being rendered of no value, she enclosed it in a large yellow envelope, sealed it, and that evening handed the envelope to Mr. Watson with the request that it be not opened until after her death.

Patricia, in her delight, whispered to the lawyer that the paper was really signed, and he was well pleased and guarded the supposed treasure carefully. The girl also took occasion to inform both Beth and Louise that a new will had been made in which they both profited largely, but she kept the secret of who the real heir was, and both her cousins grew to believe they would share equally in the entire property.

So now an air of harmony settled upon Elmhurst, and Uncle John joined the others in admiration of the girl who had conquered the stubbornness of her stern old aunt and proved herself so unselfish and true.

One morning Aunt Jane had Phibbs wheel her into her little garden, as usual, and busied herself examining the flowers and plants of which she had always been so fond.

"James has been neglecting his work, lately," she said, sharply, to her attendant.

"He's very queer, ma'am," replied old Martha, "ever since the young ladies an' Master John came to Elmhurst. Strangers he never could abide, as you know, and he runs and hides himself as soon as he sees any of 'em about."

"Poor James!" said Miss Merrick, recalling her old gardener's infirmity. "But he must not neglect my flowers in this way, or they will be ruined."

"He isn't so afraid of Master John," went on Phibbs, reflectively, "as he is of the young ladies. Sometimes Master John talks to James, in his quiet way, and I've noticed he listens to him quite respectively—like he always does to you, Miss Jane."

"Go and find James, and ask him to step

here," commanded the mistress, "and then guard
the opening in the hedge, and see that none of my
nieces appear to bother him."

Phibbs obediently started upon her errand,
and came upon James in the tool-house, at the
end of the big garden. He was working among
his flower pots and seemed in a quieter mood
than usual.

Phibbs delivered her message, and the gardener at once started to obey. He crossed the
garden unobserved and entered the little enclosure where Miss Jane's chair stood. The invalid
was leaning back on her cushions, but her eyes
were wide open and staring.

"I've come, Miss," said James; and then, getting no reply, he looked into her face. A gleam
of sunlight filtered through the bushes and fell
aslant Jane Merrick's eyes; but not a lash quiv-
ered.

James gave a scream that rang through the
air and silenced even the birds. Then, shrieking
like the madman he was, he bounded away
through the hedge, sending old Martha whirling

into a rose-bush, and fled as if a thousand fiends were at his heels.

John Merrick and Mr. Watson, who were not far off, aroused by the bloodcurdling screams, ran toward Aunt Jane's garden, and saw in a glance what had happened.

"Poor Jane," whispered the brother, bending over to tenderly close the staring eyes, "her fate has overtaken her unawares."

"Better so," said the lawyer, gently. "She has found Peace at last."

Together they wheeled her back into her chamber, and called the women to care for their dead mistress.

# CHAPTER XXI.

## READING THE WILL.

Aunt Jane's funeral was extremely simple and quiet. The woman had made no friends during her long residence in the neighborhood, having isolated herself at "the big house" and refused to communicate in any way with the families living near by. Therefore, although her death undoubtedly aroused much interest and comment, no one cared to be present at the obsequies.

So the minister came from Elmwood, and being unable to say much that was good or bad of "the woman who had departed from this vale of tears," he confined his remarks to generalities and made them as brief as possible. Then the body was borne to the little graveyard a mile away, followed by the state carriage, containing

the three nieces and Kenneth; the drag with
Silas Watson and Uncle John, the former driv-
ing; and then came the Elmhurst carryall with
the servants. James did not join these last; nor
did he appear at the house after that dreadful
scene in the garden. He had a little room over
the tool-house, which Jane Merrick had had prepared for him years ago, and here he locked himself in day and night, stealthily emerging but to
secure the food Susan carried and placed before
his door.

No one minded James much, for all the in-
mates of Elhurst were under severe and exciting
strain in the days preceding the funeral.

The girls wept a little, but it was more on
account of the solemnity following the shadow
of death than for any great affection they bore
their aunt. Patsy, indeed, tried to deliver a trib-
ute to Aunt Jane's memory; but it was not an
emphatic success.

"I'm sure she had a good heart," said the
girl, "and if she had lived more with her own
family and cultivated her friends she would have

been much less hard and selfish. At the last, you know, she was quite gentle."

"I hadn't noticed it," remarked Beth.

"Oh; I did. And she made a new will, after that awful one she told us of, and tried to be just and fair to all."

"I'm glad to hear that," said Louise. "Tell us, Patsy, what does the will say? You must know all about it."

"Mr. Watson is going to read it, after the funeral," replied the girl, "and then you will know as much about it as I do. I mustn't tell secrets, my dear."

So Louise and Beth waited in much nervous excitement for the final realization of their hopes or fears, and during the drive to the cemetary there was little conversation in the state carriage. Kenneth's sensitive nature was greatly affected by the death of the woman who had played so important a part in the brief story of his life, and the awe it inspired rendered him gloomy and silent. Lawyer Watson had once warned him that Miss Merrick's death might make him an outcast, and he felt the insecurity of his present position.

But Patsy, believing he would soon know of his good fortune, watched him curiously during the ride, and beamed upon him as frequently as her own low spirits would permit.

"You know, Ken," she reminded him, "that whatever happens we are always to remain friends."

"Of course," replied the boy, briefly.

The girl had thrown aside her crutches, by this time, and planned to return to her work immediately after the funeral.

The brief services at the cemetery being concluded, the little cavalcade returned to Elmhurst, where luncheon was awaiting them.

Then Mr. Watson brought into the drawing room the tin box containing the important Elmhurst papers in his possession, and having requested all present to be seated he said:

"In order to clear up the uncertainty that at present exists concerning Miss Merrick's last will and testament, I will now proceed to read to you the document, which will afterward be properly probated according to law."

There was no need to request their attention. An intense stillness pervaded the room.

The lawyer calmly unlocked the tin box and drew out the sealed yellow envelope which Miss Merrick had recently given him. Patsy's heart was beating with eager expectancy. She watched the lawyer break the seal, draw out the paper and then turn red and angry. He hesitated a moment, and then thrust the useless document into its enclosure and cast it aside.

"Is anything wrong?" asked the girl in a low whisper, which was yet distinctly heard by all.

Mr. Watson seemed amazed. Jane Merrick's deceitful trickery, discovered so soon after her death, was almost horrible for him to contemplate. He had borne much from this erratic woman, but had never believed her capable of such an act.

So he said, in irritable tones:

"Miss Merrick gave me this document a few days ago, leading me to believe it was her last will. I had prepared it under her instruction and understood that it was properly signed. But she has herself torn off and destroyed the signature and marked the paper 'void,' so that the will previously made is the only one that is valid."

"What do you mean?" cried Patsy, in amazement. "Isn't Kenneth to inherit Elmhurst, after all?"

"Me! Me inherit?" exclaimed the boy.

"That is what she promised me," declared Patsy, while tears of indignation stood in her eyes. "I saw her sign it, myself, and if she has fooled me and destroyed the signature she's nothing but an old fraud—and I'm glad she's dead!"

With this she threw herself, sobbing, upon a sofa, and Louise and Beth, shocked to learn that after all their cousin had conspired against them, forebore any attempt to comfort her.

But Uncle John, fully as indignant as Patricia, came to her side and laid a hand tenderly on the girl's head.

"Never mind, little one," he said. "Jane was always cruel and treacherous by nature, and we might have expected she'd deceive her friends

# AUNT JANE'S NIECES.

even in death. But you did the best you could, Patsy, dear, and it can't be helped now."

Meantime the lawyer had been fumbling in the box, and now drew out the genuine will.

"Give me your attention, please," said he.

Patsy sat up and glared at him.

"I won't take a cent of it!" she exclaimed.

"Be silent!" demanded the lawyer, sternly. "You have all, I believe, been told by Miss Merrick of the terms of this will, which is properly signed and attested. But it is my duty to read it again, from beginning to end, and I will do so."

Uncle John smiled when his bequest was mentioned, and Beth frowned. Louise, however, showed no sign of disappointment. There had been a miserable scramble for this inheritance, she reflected, and she was glad the struggle was over. The five thousand dollars would come in handy, after all, and it was that much more than she had expected to have before she received Aunt Jane's invitation. Perhaps she and her mother would use part of it for a European trip, if their future plans seemed to warrant it.

234

"As far as I am concerned," said Patsy, defiantly, "you may as well tear up this will, too. I won't have that shameful old woman's money."

"That is a matter the law does not allow you to decide," returned the lawyer, calmly. "You will note the fact that I am the sole executor of the estate, and must care for it in your interests until you are of age. Then it will be turned over to you to do as you please with."

"Can I give it away, if I want to?"

"Certainly. It is now yours without recourse, and although you cannot dispose of it until you are of legal age, there will be nothing then to prevent your transfering it to whomsoever you please. I called Miss Merrick's attention to this fact when you refused to accept the legacy."

"What did she say?"

"That you would be more wise then, and would probably decide to keep it."

Patsy turned impulsively to the boy.

"Kenneth," she said, "I faithfully promise, in the presence of these witnesses, to give you Elmhurst and all Aunt Jane's money as soon as I am of age."

AUNT JANE'S NIECES.

"Good for you, Patsy," said Uncle John.

The boy seemed bewildered.

"I don't want the money—really I don't!" he protested. "The five thousand she left me will be enough. But I'd like to live here at Elmhurst for a time, until it's sold or some one else comes to live in the house!"

"It's yours," said Patsy, with a grand air. "You can live here forever."

Mr. Watson seemed puzzled.

"If that is your wish, Miss Patricia," bowing gravely in her direction, "I will see that it is carried out. Although I am, in this matter, your executor, I shall defer to your wishes as much as possible."

"Thank you," she said and then, after a moment's reflection, she added: "Can't you give to Louise and Beth the ten thousand dollars they were to have under the other will, instead of the five thousand each that this one gives them?"

"I will consider that matter," he replied; "perhaps it can be arranged."

Patsy's cousins opened their eyes at this, and began to regard her with more friendly glances.

AUNT JANE'S NIECES.

To have ten thousand each instead of five would be a very nice thing, indeed, and Miss Patricia Doyle had evidently become a young lady whose friendship it would pay to cultivate. If she intended to throw away the inheritance, a portion of it might fall to their share.

They were expressing to Patsy their gratitude when old Donald suddenly appeared in the doorway and beckoned to Uncle John.

"Will you please come to see James, sir?" he asked. "The poor fellow's dying."

# CHAPTER XXII.

### JAMES TELLS A STRANGE STORY.

Uncle John followed the coachman up the stairs to the little room above the tool-house, where the old man had managed to crawl after old Sam had given him a vicious kick in the chest.

"Is he dead?" he asked.

"No, sir; but mortally hurt, I'm thinkin'. It must have happened while we were at the funeral."

He opened the door, outside which Susan and Oscar watched with frightened faces, and led John Merrick into the room.

James lay upon his bed with closed eyes. His shirt, above the breast, was reeking with blood.

238

"The doctor should be sent for," said Uncle John.

"He'll be here soon, for one of the staple boys rode to fetch him. But I thought you ought to know at once, sir."

"Quite right, Donald."

As they stood there the wounded man moved and opened his eyes, looking from one to the other of them wonderingly. Finally he smiled.

"Ah, it's Donald," he said.

"Yes, old friend," answered the coachman. "And this is Mr. John."

"Mr. John? Mr. John? I don't quite remember you, sir," with a slight shake of the gray head. "And Donald, lad, you've grown wonderful old, somehow."

"It's the years, Jeemes," was the reply. "The years make us all old, sooner or later."

The gardener seemed puzzled, and examined his companions more carefully. He did not seem to be suffering any pain.

Finally he sighed.

"The dreams confuse me," he said, as if to explain something. "I can't always separate

239

them, the dreams from the real. Have I been sick, Donald?"

"Yes, lad. You're sick now."

The gardener closed his eyes, and lay silent.

"Do you think he's sane?" whispered Uncle John.

"I do, sir. He's sane for the first time in years."

James looked at them again, and slowly raised his hand to wipe the damp from his forehead.

"About Master Tom," he said, falteringly. "Master Tom's dead, ain't he?"

"Yes, Jeems."

"That was real, then, an' no dream. I mind it all, now— the shriek of the whistle, the crash, and the screams of the dying. Have I told you about it, Donald?"

"No, lad."

"It all happened before we knew it. I was on one side the car and Master Tom on the other. My side was on top, when I came to myself, and Master Tom was buried in the rubbish. God knows how I got him out, but I did. Donald, the poor master's side was crushed in, and both legs splintered. I knew at once he was dying, when I carried him to the grass and laid him down; and he knew it, too. Yes, the master knew he was done; and him so young and happy, and just about to be married to—to—the name escapes me, lad!"

His voice sank to a low mumble, and he closed his eyes wearily.

The watchers at his side stood still and waited. It might be that death had overtaken the poor fellow. But no; he moved again, and opened his eyes, continuing his speech in a stronger tone.

"It was hard work to get the paper for Master Tom," he said; "but he swore he must have it before he died. I ran all the way to the station house and back—a mile or more—and brought the paper and a pen and ink, besides. It was but a telegraph blank—all I could find. Naught but a telegraph blank, lad."

Again his voice trailed away into a mumbling whisper, but now Uncle John and Donald looked into one another's eyes with sudden interest.

"He mustn't die yet!" said the little man; and the coachman leaned over the wounded form and said, distinctly:

"Yes, lad; I'm listening."

"To be sure," said James, brightening a bit. "So I held the paper for him, and the brakeman supported Master Tom's poor body, and he wrote out the will as clear as may be."

"The will!"

"Sure enough; Master Tom's last will. Isn't my name on it, too, where I signed it? And the conductor's beside it, for the poor brakeman didn't dare let him go? Of course. Who should sign the will with Master Tom but me—his old servant and friend? Am I right, Donald?"

"Yes, lad."

" 'Now,' says Master Tom, 'take it to Lawyer Watson, James, and bid him care for it. And give my love to Jane'—that's the name, Donald; the one I thought I'd forgot—'and now lay me back and let me die.' His very words, Donald. And we laid him back and he died. And he died. Poor Master Tom. Poor, poor young Master. And him to—be married—in a—"

"The paper, James!" cried Uncle John, recalling the dying man to the present. "What became of it?"

"Sir, I do not know you," answered James, suspiciously. "The paper's for Lawyer Watson. It's he alone shall have it."

"Here I am, James," cried the lawyer, thrusting the others aside and advancing to the bed. "Give me the paper. Where is it? I am Lawyer Watson!"

The gardener laughed—a horrible, croaking laugh that ended with a gasp of pain.

"*You* Lawyer Watson?" he cried, a moment later, in taunting tones. "Why, you old fool, Si Watson's as young as Master Tom—as young as I am! You—*you* Lawyer Watson! Ha, ha, ha!"

"Where is the paper?" demanded the lawyer fiercely.

James stared at him an instant, and then suddenly collapsed and fell back inert upon the bed.

# AUNT JANE'S NIECES.

"Have you heard all?" asked John Merrick, laying his hand on the lawyer's shoulder.

"Yes; I followed you here as soon as I could. Tom Bradley made another will, as he lay dying. I must have it, Mr. Merrick."

"Then you must find it yourself," said Donald gravely, "for Jemes is dead."

The doctor, arriving a few minutes later, verified the statement. It was evident that the old gardener, for years insane, had been so influenced by Miss Merrick's death that he had wandered into the stables where he received his death blow. When he regained consciousness the mania had vanished, and in a shadowy way he could remember and repeat that last scene of the tragedy that had deprived him of his reason. The story was logical enough, and both Mr. Watson and John Merrick believed it.

"Tom Bradley was a level-headed fellow until he fell in love with your sister," said the lawyer to his companion. "But after that he would not listen to reason, and perhaps he had a premonition of his own sudden death, for he made a will bequeathing all he possessed to his sweetheart. I drew up the will myself, and argued against the folly of it; but he had his own way. Afterward, in the face of death, I believe he became more sensible, and altered his will."

"Yet James' story may all be the effect of a disordered mind," said Uncle John.

"I do not think so; but unless he has destroyed the paper in his madness, we shall be able to find it among his possessions."

With this idea in mind, Mr. Watson ordered the servants to remove the gardener's body to a room in the carriage-house, and as soon as this was done he set to work to search for the paper, assisted by John Merrick.

"It was a telegraph blank, he said."

"Yes."

"Then we cannot mistake it, if we find any papers at all," declared the lawyer.

The most likely places in James' room for anything to be hidden were a small closet, in which were shelves loaded with odds and ends, and an old clothes-chest that was concealed underneath the bed.

This last was first examined, but found to

contain merely an assortment of old clothing. Having tossed these in a heap upon the floor the lawyer begun an examination of the closet, the shelves promising well because of several bundles of papers they contained.

While busy over these, he heard Uncle John say, quietly:

"I've got it."

The lawyer bounded from the closet. The little man had been searching the pockets of the clothing taken from the chest, and from a faded velvet coat he drew out the telegraph blank.

"Is it the will?" asked the lawyer, eagerly.

"Read it yourself," said Uncle John.

Mr. Watson put on his glasses.

"Yes; this is Tom Bradley's handwriting, sure enough. The will is brief, but it will hold good in law. Listen: 'I bequeath to Jane Merrick, my affianced bride, the possession and use of my estate during the term of her life. On her death all such possessions, with their accrument, shall be transferred to my sister, Katherine Bradley, if she then survives, to have and to hold by her heirs and assignees forever. But should

246

AUNT JANE'S NIECES.

she die without issue previous to the death of
Jane Merrick, I then appoint my friend and at-
torney, Silas Watson, to distribute the property
among such organized and worthy charities as
he may select.' That is all."

"Quite enough," said Uncle John, nodding
approval.

"And it is properly signed and witnessed.
The estate is Kenneth's, sir, after all, for he is
the sole heir of his mother, Katherine Bradley
Forbes. Hurrah!" ended the lawyer, waving the
yellow paper above his head.

"Hurrah!" echoed Uncle John, gleefully;
and the two men shook hands.

# CHAPTER XXIII.

Uncle John and Mr. Watson did not appear at dinner, being closeted in the former's room. This meal, however, was no longer a state function, being served by the old servants as a mere matter of routine. Indeed, the arrangements of the household had been considerably changed by the death of its mistress, and without any real head to direct them the servants were patiently awaiting the advent of a new master or mistress. It did not seem clear to them yet whether Miss Patricia or Lawyer Watson was to take charge of Elmhurst; but there were few tears shed for Jane Merrick, and the new regime could not fail to be an improvement over the last.

At dinner the young folks chatted together in a friendly and eager manner concerning the events of the day. They knew of old James' unfortunate end, but being unaware of its import gave it but passing attention. The main subject of conversation was Aunt Jane's surprising act in annulling her last will and forcing Patricia to accept the inheritance when she did not want it. Kenneth, being at his ease when alone with the three cousins, protested that it would not be right for Patsy to give him all the estate. But, as she was so generous, he would accept enough of his Uncle Tom's money to educate him as an artist and provide for himself an humble home. Louise and Beth, having at last full knowledge of their cousin's desire to increase their bequests, were openly very grateful for her good will, although secretly they could not fail to resent Patsy's choice of the boy as the proper heir of his uncle's fortune. The balance of power seemed to be in Patricia's hands, however; so it would be folly at this juncture to offend her.

Altogether, they were all better provided for than they had feared would be the case; so the little party spent a pleasant evening and separated early, Beth and Louise to go to their rooms and canvass quietly the events of the day, and the boy to take a long stroll through the country lanes to cool his bewildered brain. Patsy wrote a long letter to the major, telling him she would be home in three days, and then she went to bed and slept peacefully.

After breakfast they were all again summoned to the drawing-room, to their great surprise. Lawyer Watson and Uncle John were there, looking as grave as the important occasion demanded, and the former at once proceeded to relate the scene in James' room, his story of the death of Thomas Bradley, and the subsequent finding of the will.

"This will, which has just been recovered," continued the lawyer, impressively, "was made subsequent to the one under which Jane Merrick inherited, and therefore supercedes it. Miss Jane had, as you perceive, a perfect right to the use of the estate during her lifetime, but no right whatever to will a penny of it to anyone, Mr. Bradley having provided for that most fully. For this reason the will I read to you yesterday is of no effect, and Kenneth Forbes inherits from his uncle, through his mother, all of the estate."

Blank looks followed Mr. Watson's statement.

"Good-by to my five thousand," said Uncle John, with his chuckling laugh. "But I'm much obliged to Jane, nevertheless."

"Don't we get anything at all?" asked Beth, with quivering lip.

"No, my dear," answered the lawyer, gently. "Your aunt owned nothing to give you."

Patsy laughed. She felt wonderfully relieved.

"Wasn't I the grand lady, though, with all the fortune I never had?" she cried merrily. "But 'twas really fine to be rich for a day, and toss the money around as if I didn't have to dress ten heads of hair in ten hours to earn my bread and butter."

Louise smiled.

"It was all a great farce," she said. "I shall take the afternoon train to the city. What an old fraud our dear Aunt Jane was! And how foolish of me to return her hundred dollar check."

"I used mine," said Beth, bitterly. "It's all I'll ever get, it seems." And then the thought of the Professor and his debts overcame her and she burst into tears.

The boy sat doubled within his chair, so overcome by the extraordinary fortune that had overtaken him that he could not speak, nor think even clearly as yet.

Patsy tried to comfort Beth.

"Never mind, dear," said she. "We're no worse off than before we came, are we? And we've had a nice vacation. Let's forget all disappointments and be grateful to Aunt Jane's memory. As far as she knew, she tried to be good to us."

"I'm going home today," said Beth, angrily drying her eyes.

"We'll all go home," said Patsy, cheerfully.

"For my part," remarked Uncle John, in a grave voice, "I have no home."

Patsy ran up and put her arm around his neck.

"Poor Uncle John!" she cried. "Why, you're worse off than any of us. What's going to become of you, I wonder?"

"I'm wondering that myself," said the little man, meekly.

"Ah! You can stay here," said the boy, suddenly arousing from his apathy.

"No," replied Uncle John, "the Merricks are out of Elmhurst now, and it returns to its rightful owners. You owe me nothing, my lad."

"But I like you," said Kenneth, "and you're old and homeless. Stay at Elmhurst, and you shall always be welcome."

Uncle John seemed greatly affected, and wrung the boy's hand earnestly. But he shook his head.

"I've wandered all my life," he said. "I can wander yet."

"See here," exclaimed Patsy. "We're all three your nieces, and we'll take care of you between us. Won't we, girls?"

Louise smiled rather scornfully, and Beth scowled.

"My mother and I live so simply in our little

253

flat," said one, "that we really haven't extra room to keep a cat. But we shall be glad to assist Uncle John as far as we are able."

"Father can hardly support his own family," said the other; "but I will talk to my mother about Uncle John when I get home, and see what she says."

"Oh, you don't need to, indeed!" cried Patsy, in great indignation. "Uncle John is my dear mother's brother, and he's to come and live with the Major and me, as long as he cares to. There's room and to spare, Uncle," turning to him and clasping his hand, "and a joyful welcome into the bargain. No, no! say nothing at all, sir! Come you shall, if I have to drag you; and if you act naughty I'll send for the Major to punish you!"

Uncle John's eyes were moist. He looked on Patsy most affectionately and cast a wink at Lawyer Watson, who stood silently by.

"Thank you, my dear," said he; "but where's the money to come from?"

"Money? Bah!" she said. "Doesn't the Major earn a heap with his bookkeeping, and

254

AUNT JANE'S NIECES.

haven't I had a raise lately? Why, we'll be as
snug and contented as pigs in clover. Can you
get ready to come with me today, Uncle John?"

"Yes," he said slowly. "I'll be ready,
Patsy."

So the exodus from Elmhurst took place that
very day, and Beth travelled in one direction,
while Louise, Patsy and Uncle John took the
train for New York. Louise had a seat in the
parlor car, but Patsy laughed at such extravagance.

"It's so much easier than walking," she said
to Uncle John, "that the common car is good
enough," and the old man readily agreed with
her.

Kenneth and Mr. Watson came to the station to see them off, and they parted with many
mutual expressions of friendship and good will.

Louise, especially, pressed an urgent invitation upon the new master of Elmhurst to visit
her mother in New York, and he said he hoped
to see all the girls again. They were really like
cousins to him, by this time. And after they
were all gone he rode home on Nora's back quite

255

disconsolate, in spite of his wonderful fortune.

The lawyer, who had consented to stay at the mansion for a time, that the boy might not be lonely, had already mapped out a plan for the young heir's advancement. As he rode beside Kenneth he said:

"You ought to travel, and visit the art centers of Europe, and I shall try to find a competent tutor to go with you."

"Can't you go yourself?" asked the boy.

The lawyer hesitated.

"I'm getting old, and my clients are few and unimportant, aside from the Elmhurst interests," he said. "Perhaps I can manage to go abroad with you."

"I'd like that," declared the boy. "And we'd stop in New York, wouldn't we, for a time?"

"Of course. Do you want to visit New York especially?"

"Yes."

"It's rather a stupid city," said the lawyer, doubtfully.

"That may be," answered the boy. "But Patsy will be there, you know."

# CHAPTER XXIV.

### HOME AGAIN.

The Major was at the station to meet them. Uncle John had shyly suggested a telegram, and Patsy had decided they could stand the expense for the pleasure of seeing the old Dad an hour sooner.

The girl caught sight of him outside the gates, his face red and beaming as a poppy in bloom and his snowy moustache bristling with eagerness. At once she dropped her bundles and flew to the Major's arms, leaving the little man in her wake to rescue her belongings and follow after.

He could hardly see Patsy at all, the Major wrapped her in such an ample embrace; but bye and bye she escaped to get her breath, and then

257

her eyes fell upon the meek form holding her bundles.

"Oh, Dad," she cried, "here's Uncle John, who has come to live with us; and if you don't love him as much as I do I'll make your life miserable!"

"On which account," said the Major, grasping the little man's hand most cordially, "I'll love Uncle John like my own brother. And surely," he added, his voice falling tenderly, "my dear Violet's brother must be my own. Welcome, sir, now and always, to our little home. It's modest, sir; but wherever Patsy is the sun is sure to shine."

"I can believe that," said Uncle John, with a nod and smile.

They boarded a car for the long ride up town, and as soon as they were seated Patsy demanded the story of the Major's adventures with his colonel, and the old fellow rattled away with the eagerness of a boy, telling every detail in the most whimsical manner, and finding something humorous in every incident.

"Oh, but it was grand, Patsy!" he ex-

claimed, "and the Colonel wept on my neck when
we parted and stained the collar of me best coat,
and he give me a bottle of whiskey that would
make a teetotaler roll his eyes in ecstacy. 'Twas
the time of my life."

"And you're a dozen years younger, Major!"
she cried, laughing, "and fit to dig into work
like a pig in clover."

His face grew grave.

"But how about the money, Patsy dear?" he
asked. "Did you get nothing out of Jane Merrick's estate?"

"Not a nickle, Dad. 'Twas the best joke
you ever knew. I fought with Aunt Jane like
a pirate and it quite won her heart. When she
died she left me all she had in the world."

"Look at that, now!" said the Major, wonderingly.

"Which turned out to be nothing at all," continued Patsy. "For another will was found,
made by Mr. Thomas Bradley, which gave the
money to his own nephew after Aunt Jane died.
Did you ever?"

"Wonderful!" said the Major, with a sigh.

AUNT JANE'S NIECES.

"So I was rich for half a day, and then poor as ever."

"It didn't hurt you, did it?" asked the Major. "You weren't vexed with disappointment, were you, Patsy?"

"Not at all, Daddy."

"Then don't mind it, child. Like as not the money would be the ruination of us all. Eh, sir?" appealing to Uncle John.

"To be sure," said the little man. "Jane left five thousand to me, also, which I didn't get. But I'm not sorry at all."

"Quite right, sir," approved the Major, sympathetically, "although it's easier not to expect anything at all, than to set your heart on a thing and then not get it. In your case, it won't matter. Our house is yours, and there's plenty and to spare."

"Thank you," said Uncle John, his face grave but his eyes merry.

"Oh, Major!" cried Patsy, suddenly. "There's Danny Reeves's restaurant. Let's get off and have our dinner now; I'm as hungry as a bear."

260

# AUNT JANE'S NIECES.

So they stopped the car and descended, lugging all the parcels into the little restaurant, where they were piled into a chair while the proprietor and the waiters all gathered around Patsy to welcome her home.

My, how her eyes sparkled! She fairly danced for joy, and ordered the dinner with reckless disregard of the bill.

"Ah, but it's good to be back," said the little Bohemian, gleefully. "The big house at Elmhurst was grand and stately, Major, but there wasn't an ounce of love in the cupboard."

"Wasn't I there, Patsy?" asked Uncle John, reproachfully.

"True, but now you're here; and our love, Uncle, has nothing to do with Elmhurst. I'll bet a penny you liked it as little as I did."

"You'd win," admitted the little man.

"And now," said the girl to the smiling waiter, "a bottle of red California wine for Uncle John and the Major, and two real cigars. We'll be merry tonight if it bankrupts the Doyle family entirely."

But, after a merry meal and a good one, there was no bill at all when it was called for.

Danny Reeves himself came instead, and made a nice little speech, saying that Patsy had always brought good luck to the place, and this dinner was his treat to welcome her home.

So the Major thanked him with gracious dignity and Patsy kissed Danny on his right cheek, and then they went away happy and content to find the little rooms up the second flight of the old tenement.

"It's no palace," said Patsy, entering to throw down the bundles as soon as the Major unlocked the door, "but there's a cricket in the hearth, and it's your home, Uncle John, as well as our."

Uncle John looked around curiously. The place was so plain after the comparative luxury of Elmhurst, and especially of the rose chamber Patsy had occupied, that the old man could not fail to marvel at the girl's ecstatic joy to find herself in the old tenement again. There was one good sized living-room, with an ancient rag-carpet partially covering the floor, a sheet-iron

AUNT JANE'S NIECES.

stove, a sofa, a table and three or four old-fash-
ioned chairs that had probably come from a sec-
ond-hand dealer.

Opening from this were two closet-like
rooms containing each a bed and a chair, with a
wash-basin on a bracket shelf. On the walls
were a few colored prints from the Sunday news-
papers and one large and fine photograph of a
grizzled old soldier that Uncle John at once
decided must represent "the Colonel."

Having noted these details, Patsy's uncle
smoothed back his stubby gray hair with a re-
flective and half puzzled gesture.

"It's cozy enough, my child; and I thank you
for my welcome," said he. "But may I enquire
where on earth you expect to stow me in this
rather limited establishment?"

"Where? Have you no eyes, then?" she
asked, in astonishment. "It's the finest sofa in
the world, Uncle John, and you'll sleep there
like a top, with the dear Colonel's own picture
looking down at you to keep you safe and give
you happy dreams. Where, indeed!"

"Ah; I see," said Uncle John.

263

AUNT JANE'S NIECES.

"And you can wash in my chamber," added
the Major, with a grand air, "and hang your
clothes on the spare hooks behind my door."

"I haven't many," said Uncle John, looking
thoughtfully at his red bundle.

The Major coughed and turned the lamp a
little higher.

"You'll find the air fine, and the neighborhood respectable," he said, to turn the subject.
"Our modest apartments are cool in summer and
warm in winter, and remarkably reasonable in
price. Patsy gets our breakfast on the stove yon-
der, and we buy our lunches down town, where
we work, and then dine at Danny Reeves's place.
A model home, sir, and a happy one, as I hope
you'll find it."

"I'm sure to be happy here," said Uncle John,
taking out his pipe. "May I smoke?"

"Of course; but don't spoil the lace curtains,
dear," answered Patsy, mischievously. And
then, turning to her father, she exclaimed: "Oh,
daddy! What will the Uncle do all the day
while we're at work?"

AUNT JANE'S NIECES.

"That's as he may choose," said the Major, courteously.

"Couldn't we get him a job?" asked Patsy, wistfully. " Not where there'll be much work, you know, for the Uncle is old. But just to keep him out of mischief, and busy. He can't hang around all day and be happy, I suppose."

"I'll look around," answered the Major, briskly, as if such a "job" was the easiest thing in the world to procure. "And meantime—"

"Meantime," said Uncle John, smiling at them, "I'll look around myself."

"To be sure," agreed the Major. "Between the two of us and Patsy, we ought to have no trouble at all."

There was a moment of thoughtful silence after this, and then Patsy said:

"You know it won't matter, Uncle John, if you don't work. There'll easy be enough for all, with the Major's wages and my own."

"By the bye," added the Major, "if you have any money about you, which is just possible, sir, of course, you'd better turn it over to Patsy

265

to keep, and let her make you an allowance. That's the way I do—it's very satisfactory."

"The Major's extravagant," exclaimed Patsy; "and if he has money he wants to treat every man he meets."

Uncle John shook his head, reproachfully, at the Major.

"A very bad habit, sir," he said.

" I acknowledge it, Mr. Merrick," responded the Major. "But Patsy is fast curing me. And, after all, it's a wicked city to be carrying a fat pocketbook around in, as I've often observed."

"My pocketbook is not exactly fat," remarked Uncle John.

"But you've money, sir, for I marked you squandering it on the train," said Patsy, severely. "So out with it, and we'll count up, and see how much of an allowance I can make you 'till you get the job."

Uncle John laughed and drew his chair up to the table. Then he emptied his trousers' pockets upon the cloth, and Patsy gravely separated the keys and jackknife from the coins and proceeded to count the money.

"Seven dollars and forty-two cents," she announced. "Any more?"

Uncle John hesitated a moment, and then drew from an inner pocket of his coat a thin wallet. From this, when she had received it from his hand, the girl abstracted two ten and one five dollar bills, all crisp and new.

"Good gracious!" she cried, delightedly. "All this wealth, and you pleading poverty?"

"I never said I was a pauper," returned Uncle John, complacently.

"You couldn't, and be truthful, sir," declared the girl. "Why, this will last for ages, and I'll put it away safe and be liberal with your allowance. Let me see," pushing the coins about with her slender fingers, "you just keep the forty-two cents, Uncle John. It'll do for car-fare and a bit of lunch now and then, and when you get broke you can come to me."

"He smokes," observed the Major, significantly.

"Bah! a pipe," said Patsy. "And Bull Durham is only five cents a bag, and a bag ought to last a week. And every Saturday night, sir, you shall have a cigar after dinner, with the Major. It's it our regular practice."

"Thank you, Patsy," said Uncle John, meekly, and gathered up his forty-two cents.

"You've now a home, and a manager, sir, with money in the bank of Patsy & Company, Limited," announced the Major. "You ought to be very contented, sir."

"I am," replied Uncle John.

# CHAPTER XXV.

## UNCLE JOHN ACTS QUEERLY.

When Patsy and the Major had both departed for work on Monday morning Uncle John boarded a car and rode downtown also. He might have accompanied them part of the way, but feared Patsey might think him extravagant if she found him so soon breaking into the working fund of forty-two cents, which she charged him to be careful of.

He seemed to be in no hurry, for it was early yet, and few of the lower Broadway establishments were open. To pass the time he turned into a small restaurant and had coffee and a plate of cakes, in spite of the fact that Patsy had so recently prepared coffee over the sheet-iron stove and brought some hot buns from a near-by bakery. He was not especially hungry; but in sip-

269

ping the coffee and nibbling the cakes he passed the best part of an hour.

He smiled when he paid out twenty-five cents of his slender store for the refreshment. With five cents for car-fare he had now but twelve cents left of the forty-two Patsy had given him! Talk about the Major's extravagance: it could not be compared to Uncle John's.

Another hour was spent in looking in at the shop windows. Then, suddenly noting the time, Uncle John started down the street at a swinging pace, and presently paused before a building upon which was a sign, reading: "Isham, Marvin & Co., Bankers and Brokers." A prosperous looking place, it seemed, with a host of clerks busily working in the various departments. Uncle John walked in, although the uniformed official at the door eyed him suspiciously.

"Mr. Marvin in?" he inquired, pleasantly.

"Not arrived yet," said the official, who wore a big star upon his breast.

"I'll wait," announced Uncle John, and sat down upon a leather-covered bench.

The official strutted up and down, watching

the customers who entered the bank or departed, and keeping a sharp watch on the little man upon the bench.

Another hour passed.

Presently Uncle John jumped up and approached the official.

"Hasn't Mr. Marvin arrived yet?" he enquired, sharply.

"An hour ago," was the reply.

"Then why didn't you let me know? I want to see him."

"He's busy mornings. Has to look over the mail. He can't see you yet."

"Well, he will see me, and right away. Tell him John Merrick is here."

"Your card, sir."

"I haven't any. My name will do."

The official hesitated, and glanced at the little man's seedy garb and countryfied air. But something in the angry glance of the shrewd eye made him fear he had made a mistake. He opened a small door and disappeared.

In a moment the door burst open to allow egress to a big, red-bearded man in his shirtsleeves, who glanced around briefly and then rushed at Uncle John and shook both his hands cordially.

"My dear Mr. Merrick!" he exclaimed, "I'm delighted and honored to see you here. Come to my room at once. A great surprise and pleasure, sir! Thomas, I'm engaged!"

This last was directed at the head of the amazed porter, who, as the door slammed in his face, nodded solemnly and remarked:

"Fooled ag'in, and I might 'a' known it. Drat these 'ere billionaires! Why don't they dress like decent people?"

Uncle John had been advised by Patsy where to go for a good cheap luncheon; but he did not heed her admonition. Instead, he rode in a carriage beside the banker to a splendid club, where he was served with the finest dishes the chef could provide on short notice. Moreover, Mr. Marvin introduced him to several substantial gentlemen as "Mr. John Merrick, of Portland"; and each one bowed profoundly and declared he was "highly honored."

Yet Uncle John seemed in no way elated by

this reception. He retained his simple manner, although his face was more grave than Patsy had often seen it; and he talked with easy familiarity of preferred stocks and amalgamated interests and invested securities and many other queer things that the banker seemed to understand fully and to listen to with respectful deference.

Then they returned to the bank for another long session together, and there was quite an eager bustle among the clerks as they stretched their necks to get a glimpse of Mr. Marvin's companion.

"It's John Merrick" passed from mouth to mouth, and the uniformed official strutted from one window to another, saying:

"I showed him in myself. And he came into the bank as quiet like as anyone else would."

But he didn't go away quietly, you may be sure. Mr. Marvin and Mr. Isham both escorted their famous client to the door, where the Marvin carriage had been ordered to be in readiness for Mr. Merrick's service.

But Uncle John waived it aside disdainfully.

"I'll walk," he said. "There are some other errands to attend to."

So they shook his hand and reminded him of a future appointment and let him go his way. In a moment the great Broadway crowd had swallowed up John Merrick, and five minutes later he was thoughtfully gazing into a shop window again.

By and bye he bethought himself of the time, and took a cab uptown. He had more than the twelve cents in his pocket, now, besides the check book which was carefully hidden away in an inside pocket; so the cost of the cab did not worry him. He dismissed the vehicle near an uptown corner and started to walk hastily toward Danny Reeves's restaurant, a block away, Patsy was standing in the doorway, anxiously watching for him.

"Oh, Uncle John," she cried, as he strolled up, "I've been really worried about you; it's such a big city, and you a stranger. Do you know you're ten minutes late?"

"I'm sorry," he said, humbly; "but it's a long way here from downtown."

"Didn't you take a car?"

"No, my dear."

"Why, you fooolish old Uncle! Come in at once. The Major has been terribly excited over you, and swore you should not be allowed to wander through the streets without someone to look after you. But what could we do?"

"I'm all right," declared Uncle John, cordially shaking hands with Patsy's father. "Have you had a good day?"

"Fine," said the Major. "They'd missed me at the office, and were glad to have me back. And what do you think? I've got a raise."

"Really?" said Uncle John, seeing it was expected of him.

"For a fact. It's Patsy's doing, I've no doubt. She wheedled the firm into giving me a vacation, and now they're to pay me twelve a week instead of ten."

"Is that enough?" asked Uncle John, doubtfully.

"More than enough, sir. I'm getting old, and can't earn as much as a younger man. But

I'm pretty tough, and mean to hold onto that twelve a week as long as possible."

"What pay do you get, Patsy?" asked Uncle John.

"Almost as much as Daddy. We're dreadfully rich, Uncle John; so you needn't worry if you don't strike a job yourself all at once."

"Any luck today, sir," asked the Major, tucking a napkin under his chin and beginning on the soup.

Uncle John shook his head.

"Of course not," said Patsy, quickly. "It's too early, as yet. Don't hurry, Uncle John. Except that it'll keep you busy, there's no need for you to work at all."

"You're older than I am," suggested the Major, "and that makes it harder to break in. But there's no hurry, as Patsy says."

Uncle John did not seem to be worrying over his idleness. He kept on questioning his brother-in-law and his niece about their labors, and afterward related to them the sights he had seen in the shop windows. Of course he could not eat much after the feast he had had at luncheon, and this disturbed Patsy a little. She insisted he was tired, and carried her men away to the tenement rooms as soon as possible, where she installed them at the table to play cribbage until bed-time.

The next day Uncle John seemed to be busy enough, although of course Patsy could not know what he was doing. He visited a real-estate office, for one thing, and then telephoned Isham, Marvin & Co. and issued a string of orders in a voice not nearly so meek and mild as it was when he was in Patsy's presence. Whatever he had undertaken required time, for all during the week he left the tenement directly the Major and his daughter had gone to the city, and bustled about until it was time to meet them for dinner at the restaurant. But he was happy and in good spirits and enjoyed his evening game of cribbage with the Major exceedingly.

"You must be nearly bankrupt, by this time," said Patsy on Tuesday evening.

"It's an expensive city to live in," sighed Uncle John.

She gave him fifty cents of his money, then, and on Friday fifty cents more.

"After a time," she said, "you'll manage to get along with less. It's always harder to economize at first."

"How about the bills?" he inquired. "Don't I pay my share of them?"

"Your expenses are nothing at all," declared the Major, with a wave of his hand.

"But my dinners at Danny Reeves' place must cost a lot," protested Uncle John.

"Surely not; Patsy has managed all that for a trifle, and the pleasure of your company more than repays us for the bit of expense."

On Saturday night there was a pint of red wine for the two men, and then the weekly cigars were brought—very inexpensive ones, to be sure. The first whiff he took made Uncle John cough; but the Major smoked so gracefully and with such evident pleasure that his brother-in-law clung manfully to the cigar, and succeeded in consuming it to the end.

"Tomorrow is the day of rest," announced

Patsy, " so we'll all go for a nice walk in the parks after breakfast."

"And we sleep 'till eight o'clock, don't we, Patsy?" asked the Major.

"Of course."

"And the eggs for breakfast?"

"I've bought them already, three for a nickle. You don't care for more than one, do you, Uncle John?"

"No, my dear."

"It's our Sunday morning extra— an egg apiece. The Major is so fond of them."

"And so am I, Patsy."

"And now we'll have our cribbage and get to bed early. Heigho! but Sunday's a great day for folks that work."

# CHAPTER XXVI.

## A BUNCH OF KEYS.

Uncle John did not sleep well. Perhaps he had a guilty conscience. Anyway, he tossed about a good deal on the sofa-bed in the living-room, and wore himself out to such an extent that when Patsy got up at eight o'clock her uncle had fallen into his first sound sleep.

She never disturbed him until she had made the fire and cooked the coffee and boiled the three white eggs. By this time the Major was dressed and shaved, and he aroused Uncle John and bade him hurry into the closet and make his toilet, "so that Patsy could put the house to rights. "

Uncle John obeyed eagerly, and was ready as soon as the Major had brought the smoking rolls from the bakery. Ah, but it was a merry breakfast; and a delicious one into the bargain. Uncle John seemed hungry, and looked at the empty egg-shells regretfully.

"Next time, Patsy," he said, "you must buy six eggs."

"Look at his recklessness!" cried Patsy, laughing. "You're just as bad as the Major, every bit. If you men hadn't me for a guardian you'd be in the poorhouse in a month."

"But we have you, my dear," said Uncle John, smiling into her dancing eyes; "so we won't complain at one egg instead of two."

Just then someone pounded on the door, and the girl ran to open it. There was a messenger boy outside, looking smart and neat in his blue-and-gold uniform, and he touched his cap politely to the girl.

"Miss Patricia Doyle?"

"That's me."

"A parcel for you. Sign here, please."

Patsy signed, bothering her head the while to know what the little package contained and who could have sent it. Then the boy was gone, and she came back slowly to the breakfast table, with the thing in her hand.

"What is it, Patsy?" asked the Major, curiously.

"I'm dying to know, myself," said the girl.

Uncle John finished his coffee, looking unconcerned.

"A good way is to open it," remarked the Major.

It was a very neat package, wrapped in fine paper and sealed with red wax. Patsy turned it over once or twice, and then broke the wax and untied the cord.

A bunch of keys fell out first—seven of them, strung on a purple ribbon—and then a flat, impressive looking letter was discovered.

The Major stared open-mouthed. Uncle John leaned back in his chair and watched the girl's face.

"There's a mistake," said Patsy, quite bewildered. Then she read her name upon the wrapper, quite plainly written, and shook her head. "It's for me, all right. But what does it mean?"

AUNT JANE'S NIECES.

"Why not read the letter?" suggested the Major.

So she opened the big envelope and unfolded the stiff paper and read as follows:

"Miss Patricia Doyle, Becker's Flats, Duggan Street, New York. Dear Miss Doyle: An esteemed client of our house, who desires to remain unknown, has placed at your disposal the furnished apartments "D," at 3708 Willing Square, for the period of three years, or as long thereafter as you may care to retain them. Our client begs you to consider everything the apartments contain as your own, and to use it freely as it may please you. All rentals and rates are paid in advance, and you are expected to take possession at once. Moreover, our firm is commanded to serve you in any and every way you may require, and it will be our greatest pleasure to be of use to you. The keys to the apartments are enclosed herewith.

"Most respectfully,
"Isham, Marvin & Co."

Having read this to the end, in a weak voice and with many pauses, Miss Patricia Doyle

283

sat down in her chair with strange abruptness and stared blankly at her father. The Major stared back. So did Uncle John, when her eyes roved toward his face.

Patricia turned the keys over, and jingled them. Then she referred to the letter again.

"Apartments D, at 3708 Willing Square. Where's that?"

The Major shook his head. So did Uncle John.

"Might look in a directory" suggested the latter, uncertainly.

"Of course," added the Major.

"But what does it all mean?" demanded Patsy, with sudden fierceness. "Is it a joke? Isham, Marvin & Co., the great bankers! What do I know of them, or they of me?"

"That isn't the point," observed the Major, reflectively. "Who's their unknown and mysterious client? That's the question."

"To be sure," said Uncle John. "They're only the agents. You must have a fairy godmother, Patsy."

She laughed at the idea, and shook her head.

284

## AUNT JANE'S NIECES.

"They don't exist in these days, Uncle John. But the whole thing must be a joke, and nothing more."

"We'll discover that," asserted the Major, shrewdly scrutinizing the letter, which he had taken from Patsy's hands. "It surely looks genuine enough, on the face of it. I've seen the bank letter-head before, and this is no forgery, you can take my word. Get your things on, Patsy. Instead of walking in the park we'll hunt up Willing Square, and we'll take the keys with us."

"A very good idea," said Uncle John. "I'd like to go with you, if I may."

"Of course you may," answered the girl. "You're one of the family now, Uncle John, and you must help us to unravel the mystery."

The Major took off his carpet slippers and pulled on his boots, while Patricia was getting ready for the walk. Uncle John wandered around the room aimlessly for a time, and then took off his black tie and put on the white one.

Patsy noticed this, when she came out of her closet, and laughed merrily.

"You mustn't be getting excited, Uncle John, until we see how this wonderful adventure turns out," she said. "But I really must wash and iron that necktie for you, if you're going to wear it on Sundays."

"Not a bad idea," said the Major. "But come, are we all ready?"

They walked down the rickety steps very gravely and sedately, Patsy jingling the keys as they went, and made their way to the corner drug store, where the Major searched in the directory for Willing Square.

To his surprise it proved to be only a few blocks away.

"But it's in the dead swell neighborhood," he explained, "where I have no occasion to visit. We can walk it in five minutes."

Patsy hesitated.

"Really, it's no use going, Dad," she protested. "It isn't in reason that I'd have a place presented me in a dead swell neighborhood. Now, is it?"

"We'll have to go, just the same," said Uncle

John. "I couldn't sleep a wink tonight it we
didn't find out what this all means."

"True enough," agreed the Major. "Come
along, Patsy; it's this way."

Willing Square was not very big, but it was
beautiful with flowers and well tended and
3807 proved to be a handsome building with a
white marble front, situated directly on a corner.
The Major examined it critically from the sidewalk, and decided it contained six suites of apartments, three on each side.

"D must be the second floor to the right,"
he said, "and that's a fine location, sure enough."

A porter appeared at the front door, which
stood open, and examined the group upon the
sidewalk with evident curiosity.

Patsy walked up to him, and ignoring the
big gold figures over the entrance she enquired:

"Is this 3807 Willing Square?"

"Yes, Miss," answered the porter; "are you
Miss Doyle?"

"I am," she answered, surprised.

"One flight up, Miss, and turn to the right,"
he continued, promptly; and then he winked over

the girl's head at Uncle John, who frowned so terribly that the man drew aside and disappeared abruptly. The Major and Patsy were staring at one another, however, and did not see this by-play.

"Let's go up," said the Major, in a husky voice, and proceeded to mount the stairs.

Patsy followed close behind, and then came Uncle John. One flight up they paused at a door marked "D", upon the panel of which was a rack bearing a card printed with the word "Doyle."

"Well, well!" gasped the Major. "Who'd have thought it, at all at all!"

Patsy, with trembling fingers, put a key in the lock, and after one or two efforts opened the door.

The sun was shining brilliantly into a tiny reception hall, furnished most luxuriously.

The Major placed his hat on the rack, and Uncle John followed suit.

No one spoke a word as they marched in humble procession into the living-room, their feet pressing without sound into the thick rugs.

# AUNT JANE'S NIECES.

Eveything here was fresh and new, but selected
with excellent taste and careful attention to detail. Not a thing was lacking, from the pretty
upright piano to the enameled clock ticking upon
the mantel. The dining-room was a picture, indeed, with stained-glass windows casting their
soft lights through the draperies and the side-
board shining with silver and glass. There was
a cellarette in one corner, the Major noticed, and
it was well stocked.

Beyond was a pantry with well filled shelves
and then the kitchen—this last filled with every
article that could possibly be needed. In a store-
room were enough provisions to stock a grocery-
store and Patsy noted with amazement that there
was ice in the refrigerator, with cream and milk
and butter cooling beside it.

They felt now as if they were intruding in
some fairy domain. It was all exquisite, though
rather tiny; but such luxury was as far removed
from the dingy rooms they had occupied as could
well be imagined. The Major coughed and
ahemmed continually; Patsy ah'd and oh'd and
seemed half frightened; Uncle John walked after

them silently, but with a pleased smile that was almost childish upon his round and rugged face.

Across the hall were three chambers, each with a separate bath, while one had a pretty dressing-room added.

".This will be Patsy's room," said the Major, with a vast amount of dignity.

"Of course," said Uncle John. "The pins on the cushion spell 'Patricia,' don't they?"

"So they do!" cried Patsy, greatly delighted.

"And this room," continued the Major, passing into the next, "will be mine. There are fine battle-scenes on the wall; and I declare, there's just the place for the colonel's photograph over the dresser!"

"Cigars, too," said Patsy, opening a little cabinet; "but 'twill be a shame to smoke in this palace."

"Then I won't live here!" declared the Major, stoutly, but no one heeded him.

"Here is Uncle John's room," exclaimed the girl, entering the third chamber.

"Mine?" enquired Uncle John in mild surprise.

"Sure, sir; you're one of the family, and I'm glad it's as good as the Major's, every bit."

Uncle John's eyes twinkled.

"I hope the bed is soft," he remarked, pressing it critically.

"It's as good as the old sofa, any day," said Patsy, indignantly.

Just then a bell tinkled, and after looking at one another in silent consternation for a moment, the Major tiptoed stealthily to the front door, followed by the others.

"What'll we do?" asked Patsy, in distress.

"Better open it," suggested Uncle John, calmly.

The Major did so, and there was a little maid bowing and smiling outside. She entered at once, closing the door behind her, and bowed again.

"This is my new mistress, I suppose," she said, looking at Patsy. "I am your servant, Miss Patricia."

Patsy gasped and stared at her. The maid was not much older than she was, but she looked pleasant and intelligent and in keeping with the rooms. She wore a gray dress with white collar and white apron and cap, and seemed so dainty and sweet that the Major and Uncle John approved her at once.

Patsy sat down, from sheer lack of strength to stand up.

"Who hired you, then?" she asked.

"A gentleman from the bank," was the reply. "I'm Mary, if you please, Miss. And my wages are all arranged for in advance, so there will be nothing for you to pay," said the little maid.

"Can you cook?" asked Patsy, curiously.

"Yes, Miss," with a smile. "The dinner will be ready at one o'clock."

"Oh; you've been here before, then?"

"Two days, Miss, getting ready for you."

"And where will you sleep?"

"I've a little room beyond the kitchen. Didn't you see it, Miss Patricia?"

"No, Mary."

"Anything more at present, Miss Patricia?"

"No, Mary."

The maid bowed again, and disappeared toward the kitchen, leaving an awe-struck group behind her.

The Major whistled softly. Uncle John seemed quite unconcerned. Patsy took out her handkerchief. The tears *would* come in spite of her efforts.

"I—I—I'm going to have a good cry," she sobbed, and rushed into the living-room to throw herself flat upon the divan.

"It's all right," said the Major, answering Uncle John's startled look; "the cry will do her good. I've half a mind to join her myself."

But he didn't. He followed Uncle John into the latter's room and smoked one of the newly-discovered cigars while the elder man lay back in an easy chair and silently puffed his pipe.

By and bye Patsy joined them, no longer crying but radiant with glee.

"Tell me, Daddy," said she, perching on the arm of the Major's chair, "who gave me all this, do you think?"

"Not me," answered the Major, positively. "I couldn't do it on twelve a week, anyhow at all."

"And you robbed me of all my money when I came to town," said Uncle John.

"Stop joking," said the girl. "There's no doubt this place is intended for us, is there?"

"None at all," declared the Major. "It's ours for three years, and not a penny to pay."

"Well, then, do you think it's Kenneth?"

The Major shook his head.

"I don't know the lad," he said, " and he might be equal to it, although I doubt it. But he can't touch his money till he comes of age, and it isn't likely his lawyer guardian would allow such extravagances."

"Then who can it be?"

"I can't imagine."

"It doesn't seem to matter," remarked Uncle John, lighting a fresh pipe. "You're not supposed to ask questions, I take it, but to enjoy your new home as much as you can."

"Ex—actly!" agreed the Major.

"I've been thinking," continued Uncle John, "that I'm not exactly fit for all this style, Patsy. I'll have to get a new suit of clothes to match my new quarters. Will you give me back ten dollars of that money to buy 'em with?"

"I suppose I'll have to," she answered, thoughtfully.

"We'll have to go back to Becker's flats to pack up our traps," said the Major, "so we might as well go now."

"I hate to leave here for a single moment," replied the girl.

"Why?"

"I'm afraid it will all disappear again."

"Nonsense!" said Uncle John. "For my part, I haven't any traps, so I'll stay here and guard the treasure till you return."

"Dinner is served, Miss Patricia," said the small maid, appearing in the doorway.

"Then let's dine!" cried Patsy, clapping her hands gleefully; "and afterward the Major and I will make our last visit to Becker's flats."

# CHAPTER XXVII.

## LOUISE MAKES A DISCOVERY.

Uncle John did not stay to guard the treasure, after all, for he knew very well it would not disappear.

As soon as Patsy and the Major had departed for Becker's flats, he took his own hat from the rack and walked away to hunt up another niece, Miss Louise Merrick, whose address he had casually obtained from Patsy a day or two before.

It was near by, and he soon found the place—a pretty flat in a fashionable building, although not so exclusive a residence district as Willing Square.

Up three flights he rode in the elevator, and then rang softly at the door which bore the card of Mrs. Merrick.

A maid opened it and looked at him enquiringly.

"Are the ladies in?" he asked.

"I'll see. Your card, sir?"

"I haven't any."

She half closed the door.

"Any name, then?"

"Yes, John Merrick."

She closed the door entirely, and was gone several minutes. Then she came back and ushered him through the parlor into a small rear room.

Mrs. Merrick arose from her chair by the window and advanced to meet him.

"You are John Merrick?" she enquired.

"Your husband's brother, ma'am," he replied.

"How do you do, Uncle John?" called Louise, from the sofa. "Excuse my getting up, won't you? And where in the world have you come from?"

Mrs. Merrick sat down again.

"Won't you take a chair?" she said, stiffly.

"I believe I will," returned Uncle John. "I just came to make a call, you know."

"Louise has told me of you," said the lady. "It was very unfortunate that your sister's death deprived you of a home. An absurd thing, altogether, that fiasco of Jane Merrick's."

"True," he agreed.

"But I might have expected it, knowing the woman's character as I did."

Uncle John wondered what Jane's character had to do with the finding of Tom Bradley's last will; but he said nothing.

"Where are you living?" asked Louise.

"Not anywhere, exactly," he answered, "although Patsy has offered me a home and I've been sleeping on a sofa in her living-room, the past week."

"I advise you to stay with the Doyles," said Mrs. Merrick, quickly. "We haven't even a sofa to offer you here, our flat is so small; otherwise we would be glad to be of some help to you. Have you found work?"

"I haven't tried to, yet, ma'am."

"It will be hard to get, at your age, of course.

But that is a matter in which we cannot assist you."

"Oh, I'm not looking for help, ma'am."

She glanced at his worn clothing and soiled white necktie, and smiled.

"But we want to do something for you," said Louise. "Now," sitting up and regarding him gravely, "I'm going to tell you a state secret. We are living, in this luxurious way, on the principal of my father's life insurance. At our present rate of expenditure we figure that the money will last us two years and nine months longer. By that time I shall be comfortably married or we will go bankrupt—as the fates decide. Do you understand the situation?"

"Perfectly. It's very simple," said the old man.

"And rather uncertain, isn't it? But in spite of this, we are better able to help you than any of your other relatives. The Doyles are hard-working folks, and very poor. Beth says that Professor De Graf is over head and ears in debt and earns less every year, so he can't be counted upon. In all the Merrick tribe the only tangible thing is my father's life insurance, which I believe you once helped him to pay a premium on."

"I'd forgotten that," said Uncle John.

"Well, we haven't. We don't want to appear ungenerous in your eyes. Some day we may need help ourselves. But just now we can't offer you a home, and, as mother says, you'd better stay with the Doyles. We have talked of making you a small allowance; but that may not be necessary. When you need assistance you must come to us, and we'll do whatever we can, as long as our money lasts. Won't that be the better way?"

Uncle John was silent for a moment. Then he asked:

"Why have you thought it necessary to assist me?"

Louise seemed surprised.

"You are old and seemed to be without means," she answered, "and that five thousand Aunt Jane left to you turned out to be a myth. But tell me, have you money, Uncle John?"

"Enough for my present needs," he said, smiling.

AUNT JANE'S NIECES.

Mrs. Merrick seemed greatly relieved.

"Then there is no need of our trying to be generous," she said, "and I am glad of that on all accounts."

"I just called for a little visit," said Uncle John. "It seemed unfriendly not to hunt you up, when I was in town."

"I'm glad you did," replied Mrs. Merrick, glancing at the clock. "But Louise expects a young gentleman to call upon her in a few minutes, and perhaps you can drop in again; another Sunday, for instance."

"Perhaps so," said Uncle John, rising with a red face. "I'll see."

"Good bye, Uncle," exclaimed Louise, rising to take his hand. "Don't feel that we've hurried you away, but come in again, whenever you feel like it."

"Thank you, my dear," he said, and went away.

Louise approached the open window, that led to a broad balcony. The people in the next flat —young Mr. Isham, the son of the great banker, and his wife—were sitting on the balcony, over-

looking the street, but Louise decided to glance
over the rail to discover if the young gentleman
she so eagerly awaited chanced to be in sight.

As she did so Mr. Isham cried in great excitement:

"There he is, Myra—that's him!" and pointed
toward the sidewalk.

"Whom?" enquired Mrs. Isham, calmly.

"Why John Merrick! John Merrick, of
Portland, Oregon."

"And who is John Merrick?" asked the lady.

"One of the richest men in the world, and the
best client our house has. Isn't he a queer looking fellow? And dresses like a tramp. But he's
worth from eighty to ninety millions, at least,
and controls most of the canning and tin-plate
industries of America. I wonder what brought
him into this neighborhood?"

Louise drew back from the window, pale and
trembling. Then she caught up a shawl and
rushed from the room. Uncle John must be
overtaken and brought back, at all hazards.

The elevator was coming down, fortunately,
and she descended quickly and reached the

street, where she peered eagerly up and down for the round, plump figure of the little millionaire. But by some strange chance he had already turned a corner and disappeared.

While she hesitated the young man came briskly up, swinging his cane.

"Why, Miss Louise," he said in some surprise, "were you, by good chance, waiting for me?"

"No, indeed," she answered, with a laugh; "I've been saying good-bye to my rich uncle, John Merrick, of Portland, who has just called."

"John Merrick, the tin-plate magnate? Is he your uncle?"

"My father's own brother," she answered, gaily. "Come upstairs, please. Mother will be glad to see you!"

# CHAPTER XXVIII.

## PATSY LOSES HER JOB.

Uncle John reached Willing Square before Patsy and her father returned, but soon afterward they arrived in an antiquated carriage surrounded by innumerable bundles.

"The driver's a friend of mine," explained the Major, "and he moved us for fifty cents, which is less than half price. We didn't bring a bit of the furniture or beds, for there's no place here to put them; but as the rent at Becker's flat is paid to the first of next month, we'll have plenty of time to auction 'em all off."

The rest of the day was spent most delightfully in establishing themselves in the new home. It didn't take the girl long to put her few belongings into the closets and drawers, but there were a thousand little things to examine in the

304

rooms, and she made some important discovery at every turn.

"Daddy," she said, impressively, "it must have cost a big fortune to furnish these little rooms. They're full of very expensive things, and none of the grand houses Madam Borne has sent me to is any finer than ours. I'm sure the place is too good for us, who are working people. Do you think we ought to stay here?"

"The Doyles," answered the Major, very seriously, "are one of the greatest and most aristocratic families in all Ireland, which is the most aristocratic country in the world. If I only had our pedigree I could prove it to you easily. There's nothing too good for an Irish gentleman, even if he condescends to bookkeeping to supply the immediate necessities of life; and as you're me own daughter, Patricia, though a Merrick on your poor sainted mother's side, you're entitled to all you can get honestly. Am I right, Uncle John, or do I flatter myself?"

Uncle John stroked the girl's head softly.

"You are quite right," he said. "There is

nothing too good for a brave, honest girl who's heart is in the right place."

"And that's Patsy," declared the Major, as if the question were finally settled.

On Monday morning Mary had a dainty breakfast all ready for th_ n at seven o'clock, and Patsy and her father departed with light hearts for their work. Uncle John rode part way down town with them.

"I'm going to buy my new suit, today, and a new necktie," he said.

"Don't let them rob you," was Patsy's parting injunction. "Is your money all safe? And if you buy a ten dollar suit of clothes the dealer ought to throw in the necktie to bind the bargain. And see that they're all wool, Uncle John."

"What, the neckties?"

"No, the clothes. Good-bye, and don't be late to dinner. Mary might scold."

"I'll remember. Good-bye, my dear."

Patsy was almost singing for joy when she walked into Madam Borne's hair-dressing establishment.

'Don't take off your things," said the Madam, sharply. "You're services are no longer required."

Patsy looked at her in amazement. Doubtless she hadn't heard aright.

"I have another girl in your place," continued Madam Borne, "so I'll bid you good morning."

Patsy's heart was beating fast.

"Do you mean I'm discharged?" she asked, with a catch in her voice.

"That's it precisely."

"Have I done anything wrong, Madam?"

"It isn't that," said Madam, pettishly. "I simply do not require your services. You are paid up to Saturday night, and I owe you nothing. Now, run along."

Patsy stood looking at her and wondering what to do. To lose this place was certainly a great calamity.

"You'll give me a testimonial, won't you, Madam?" she asked, falteringly.

"I don't give testimonials," was the reply.

## AUNT JANE'S NIECES.

"Do run away, child; I'm very busy this morning."

Patsy went away, all her happiness turned to bitter grief. What would the Major say, and what were they to do without her wages? Then she remembered Willing Square, and was a little comforted. Money was not as necessary now as it had been before.

Nevertheless, she applied to one or two hairdressers for employment, and met with abrupt refusals. They had all the help they needed. So she decided to go back home and think it over, before taking further action.

It was nearly ten o'clock when she fitted her pass-key into the carved door of Apartment D, and when she entered the pretty living-room she found an elderly lady seated there, who arose to greet her.

"Miss Doyle?" enquired the lady.

"Yes, ma'am," said Patsy.

"I am Mrs. Wilson, and I have been engaged to give you private instruction from ten to twelve every morning."

Patsy plumped down upon a chair and looked her amazement.

"May I ask who engaged you?" she ventured to enquire.

"A gentleman from the bank of Isham, Marvin & Co. made the arrangement. May I take off my things?"

"If you please," said the girl, quietly. Evidently this explained why Madam Borne had discharged her so heartlessly. The gentleman from Isham, Marvin & Co. had doubtless interviewed the Madam and told her what to do. And then, knowing she would be at liberty, he had sent her this private instructor.

The girl felt that the conduct of her life had been taken out of her own hands entirely, and that she was now being guided and cared for by her unknown friend and benefactor. And although she was inclined to resent the loss of her independence, at first, her judgment told her it would not only be wise but to her great advantage to submit.

She found Mrs. Wilson a charming and cultivated lady, who proved so gracious and kindly that the girl felt quite at ease in her presence. She soon discovered how woefully ignorant Patsy was, and arranged a course of instruction that would be of most benefit to her.

"I have been asked to prepare you to enter a girls' college," she said, "and if you are attentive and studious I shall easily accomplish the task."

Patsy invited her to stay to luncheon, which Mary served in the cosy dining-room, and then Mrs. Wilson departed and left her alone to think over this new example of her unknown friend's thoughtful care.

At three o'clock the door-bell rang and Mary ushered in another strange person—a pretty, fair-haired young lady, this time, who said she was to give Miss Doyle lessons on the piano.

Patsy was delighted. It was the one accomplishment she most longed to acquire, and she entered into the first lesson with an eagerness that made her teacher smile approvingly.

Meantime the Major was having his own surprises. At the office the manager met him on his arrival and called him into his private room.

"Major Doyle," said he, "it is with great

regret that we part with you, for you have
served our house most faithfully."

The Major was nonplussed.

"But," continued the manager, "our bankers,
Messers. Isham, Marvin & Co., have asked us to
spare you for them, as they have a place requir-
ing a man of your abilities where you can do
much better than with us. Take this card, sir,
and step over to the bankers and enquire for Mr.
Marvin. I congratulate you, Major Doyle, on
your advancement, which I admit is fully de-
served."

The Major semed dazed. Like a man walking in a dream he made his way to the great
banking house, and sent in the card to Mr. Marvin.

That gentleman greeted him most cordially.

"We want you to act as special auditor of accounts," said he. "It is a place of much re-
sponsibility, but your duties will not be arduous.
You will occupy Private Office No. 11, and your
hours are only from 10 to 12 each morning.
After that you will be at liberty. The salary, I
regret to say, is not commensurate with your

value, being merely twenty-four hundred a year; but as you will have part of the day to yourself you will doubtless be able to supplement that sum in other ways. Is this satisfactory, sir?"

"Quite so," answered the Major. Twenty-four hundred a year! And only two hours' work! Quite satisfactory, indeed!

His little office was very cosy, too; and the work of auditing the accounts of the most important customers of the house required accuracy but no amount of labor. It was an ideal occupation for a man of his years and limited training.

He stayed in the office until two o'clock that day, in order to get fully acquainted with the details of his work. Then he closed his desk, went to luncheon, which he enjoyed amazingly, and then decided to return to Willing Square and await Patsy's return from Madam Borne's.

As he let himself in he heard an awkward drumming and strumming on the piano, and peering slyly through the opening in the portierre he was startled to find Patsy herself making the dreadful noise, while a pretty girl sat beside her directing the movements of her fingers.

The Major watched for several minutes, in silent but amazed exultation; then he tip-toed softly to his room to smoke a cigar and wait until his daughter was at liberty to hear his great news and explain her own adventures.

When Uncle John came home to dinner he found father and daughter seated happily together in a loving embrace, their faces wreathed with ecstatic smiles that were wonderful to behold.

Uncle John was radiant in a brand new pepper-and-salt suit of clothes that fitted his little round form perfectly. Patsy marvelled that he could get such a handsome outfit for the money, for Uncle John had on new linen and a new hat and even a red-bordered handkerchief for the coat pocket—besides the necktie, and the necktie was of fine silk and in the latest fashion.

The transformation was complete, and Uncle John had suddenly become an eminently respectable old gentleman, with very little to criticise in his appearance.

"Do I match the flat, now?" he asked.

313

"To a dot!" declared Patsy. "So come to dinner, for it's ready and waiting, and the Major and I have some wonderful fairy tales to tell you."

# CHAPTER XXIX.

## THE MAJOR DEMANDS AN EXPLANATION.

That was a happy week, indeed. Patsy devoted all her spare time to her lessons, but the house itself demanded no little attention. She would not let Mary dust the ornaments or arrange the rooms at all, but lovingly performed those duties herself, and soon became an ideal housekeeper, as Uncle John approvingly remarked.

And as she flitted from room to room she sang such merry songs that it was a delight to hear her, and the Major was sure to get home from the city in time to listen to the strumming of the piano at three o'clock, from the recess of his own snug chamber.

Uncle John went to the city every morning, and at first this occasioned no remark. Patsy was too occupied to pay much attention to her uncle's coming and going, and the Major was indifferent, being busy admiring Patsy's happiness and congratulating himself on his own good fortune.

The position at the bank had raised the good man's importance several notches. The clerks treated him with fine consideration and the heads of the firm were cordial and most pleasant. His fine, soldierly figure and kindly, white-moustached face, conferred a certain dignity upon his employers, which they seemed to respect and appreciate.

It was on Wednesday that the Major encountered the name of John Merrick on the books. The account was an enormous one, running into millions in stocks and securities. The Major smiled.

"That's Uncle John's name," he reflected. "It would please him to know he had a namesake so rich as this one."

The next day he noted that John Merrick's holdings were mostly in western canning industries and tin-plate factories, and again he recol-

lected that Uncle John had once been a tinsmith. The connection was rather curious.

But it was not until Saturday morning that
the truth dawned upon him, and struck him like
a blow from a sledge-hammer.

He had occasion to visit Mr. Marvin's private office, but being told that the gentleman
was engaged with an important customer, he
lingered outside the door, waiting.

Presently the door was partly opened.

"Don't forget to sell two thousand of the
Continental stock tomorrow," he heard a familiar
voice say.

"I'll not forget, Mr. Merrick," answered the
banker.

"And buy that property on Bleeker street at
the price offered. It's a fair proposition, and I
need the land."

"Very well, Mr. Merrick. Would it not be
better for me to send these papers by a messenger
to your house?"

"No; I'll take them myself. No one will rob
me." And then the door swung open and, chuckling in his usual whimsical fashion, Uncle John

AUNT JANE'S NIECES.

came out, wearing his salt-and-pepper suit and
stuffing a bundle of papers into his inside pocket.

The Major stared at him, haughtily, but
made no attempt to openly recognize the man.
Uncle John gave a start, laughed, and then
walked away briskly, throwing a hasty "good-
bye" to the obsequious banker, who followed him
out, bowing low.

The Major returned to his office with a grave
face, and sat for the best part of three hours in
a brown study. Then he took his hat and went
home.

Patsy asked anxiously if anything had happened, when she saw his face; but the Major
shook his head.

Uncle John arrived just in time for dinner,
in a very genial mood, and he and Patsy kept up
a lively conversation at the table while the Major
looked stern every time he caught the little man's
eye.

But Uncle John never minded. He was not
even as meek and humble as usual, but laughed
and chatted with the freedom of a boy just out
of school, which made Patsy think the new

clothes had improved him in more ways than one.

When dinner was over the Major led them into the sitting-room, turned up the lights, and then confronted the little man with a determined and majestic air.

"Sir," said he, "give an account of your-self."

"Eh?"

"John Merrick, millionaire and impostor, who came into my family under false pretenses and won our love and friendship when we didn't know it, give an account of yourself!"

Patsy laughed.

"What are you up to, Daddy?" she demanded. "What has Uncle John been doing?"

"Deceiving us, my dear."

"Nonsense," said Uncle John, lighting his old briar pipe, "you've been deceiving yourselves."

"Didn't you convey the impression that you were poor?" demanded the Major, sternly.

"No."

"Didn't you let Patsy take away your thirty-two dollars and forty-two cents, thinking it was all you had?"

"Yes."

"Aren't you worth millions and millions of dollars—so many that you can't count them yourself?"

"Perhaps."

"Then, sir," concluded the Major, mopping the perspiration from his forehead and sitting down limply in his chair, "what do you mean by it?"

Patsy stood pale and trembling, her round eyes fixed upon her uncle's composed face.

"Uncle John!" she faltered.

"Yes, my dear."

"Is it all true? Are you so very rich?"

"Yes, my dear."

"And it's you that gave me this house, and—and everything else— and got the Major his fine job, and me discharged, and—and—"

"Of course, Patsy. Why not?"

"Oh, Uncle John!"

She threw herself into his arms, sobbing happily as he clasped her little form to his bosom. And the Major coughed and blew his nose, and muttered unintelligible words into his handkerchief. Then Patsy sprang up and rushed upon her father, crying:

"Oh, Daddy! Aren't you glad it's Uncle John?"

"I have still to hear his explanation," said the Major.

Uncle John beamed upon them. Perhaps he had never been so happy before in all his life.

"I'm willing to explain," he said, lighting his pipe again and settling himself in his chair. "But my story is a simple one, dear friends, and not nearly so wonderful as you may imagine. My father had a big family that kept him poor, and I was a tinsmith with little work to be had in the village where we lived. So I started west, working my way from town to town, until I got to Portland, Oregon.

"There was work in plenty there, making the tin cans in which salmon and other fish is packed, and as I was industrious I soon had a shop of my own, and supplied cans to the packers. The shop grew to be a great factory, employing hundreds of men. Then I bought up the factories of my competitors, so as to control the market, and as I used so much tin-plate I became interested in the manufacture of this product, and invested a good deal of money in the production and perfection of American tin. My factories were now scattered all along the coast, even to California, where I made the cans for the great quantities of canned fruits they ship from that section every year. Of course the business made me rich, and I bought real estate with my extra money, and doubled my fortune again and again.

"I never married, for all my heart was in the business, and I thought of nothing else. But a while ago a big consolidation of the canning industries was effected, and the active management I resigned to other hands, because I had grown old, and had too much money already.

"It was then that I remembered the family, and went back quietly to the village where I was born. They were all dead or scattered, I found; but because Jane had inherited a fortune in some way I discovered where she lived and went to see her. I suppose it was because my clothes were old and shabby that Jane concluded I was a poor man and needed assistance; and I didn't take the trouble to undeceive her.

"I also found my three nieces at Elmhurst, and it struck me it would be a good time to study their characters; for like Jane I had a fortune to leave behind me, and I was curious to find out which girl was the most deserving. No one suspected my disguise. I don't usually wear such poor clothes, you know; but I have grown to be careless of dress in the west, and finding that I was supposed to be a poor man I clung to that old suit like grim death to a grasshopper."

"It was very wicked of you," said Patsy, soberly, from her father's lap.

"As it turned out," continued the little man, "Jane's desire to leave her money to her nieces amounted to nothing, for the money wasn't hers. But I must say it was kind of her to put me down for five thousand dollars—now, wasn't it?"

The Major grinned.

"And that's the whole story, my friends. After Jane's death you offered me a home—the best you had to give—and I accepted it. I had to come to New York anyway, you know, for

Isham, Marvin & Co. have been my bankers for
years, and there was considerable business to
transact with them. I think that's all, isn't it?"

"Then this house is yours?" said Patsy, wonderingly.

"No, my dear; the whole block belongs to
you and here's the deed for it," drawing a package of papers from his pocket. "It's a very good
property, Patsy, and the rents you get from the
other five flats will be a fortune in themselves."

For a time the three sat in silence. Then the
girl whispered, softly:

"Why are you so good to me, Uncle John?"

"Just because I like you, Patsy, and you are
my niece."

"And the other nieces?"

"Well, I don't mean they shall wait for my
death to be made happy," answered Uncle John.
"Here's a paper that gives to Louise's mother
the use of a hundred thousand dollars, as long as
she lives. After that Louise will have the money
to do as she pleases with."

"How fine!" cried Patsy, clapping her hands
joyfully.

# AUNT JANE'S NIECES.

"And here's another paper that gives Professor De Graf the use of another hundred thousand. Beth is to have it when he dies. She's a sensible girl, and will take good care of it."

"Indeed she will!" said Patsy.

"And now," said Uncle John, "I want to know if I can keep my little room in your apartments, Patsy; or if you'd prefer me to find another boarding place."

"Your home is here as long as you live, Uncle John. I never meant to part with you, when I thought you poor, and I'll not desert you now that I know you're rich."

"Well said, Patsy!" cried the Major.

And Uncle John smiled and kissed the girl and then lighted his pipe again, for it had gone out.

*Exhilarating Books for Girls of Today*

# The Flying Girl Series

*By* EDITH VAN DYNE

*Author of "Aunt Jane's Nieces" Series*

CAPITAL up-to-the-minute stories for girls and young people, in which the author is at her very best. Thrilling and full of adventure, but of that wholesome type parents are glad to put in the hands of their daughters. Two titles:

## The Flying Girl

Orissa Kane, self-reliant and full of sparkling good nature, under-study for her brother, prospective inventor and aviator whose experiments put the Kane family into great difficulties, in the crisis proves resourceful and plucky, and saves the day in a most thrilling manner.

## The Flying Girl and Her Chum

This story takes Orissa and her friend Sybil through further adventures that test these two clever girls to the limit. A remarkably well told story.

*12mo. Bound in extra cloth with design stamping on cover and fancy jacket. Printed on high grade paper. Illustrated in black and white.*

*Price 60 cents each. Postage 12 cents.*

Publishers    The Reilly & Britton Co.    Chicago

Printed in the United States
1082700002B